WITHDRAWN

PRETTY

BY JUSTIN SAYRE

Penguin Workshop

PENGUIN WORKSHOP
Penguin Young Readers Group
An Imprint of Penguin Random House LLC

Copyright © 2017 by Justin Sayre. All rights reserved. First published in hardcover by
Grosset & Dunlap. This paperback edition published in 2018 by Penguin Workshop,
an imprint of Penguin Random House, 345 Hudson Street, New York, New York 10014.
PENGUIN and PENGUIN WORKSHOP are trademarks of Penguin Books Ltd,
and the W colophon is a trademark of Penguin Random House LLC. Printed in the USA.

The Library of Congress has cataloged the hardcover edition under the following
Control Number: 2017950976

ISBN 9780448484181 | 10 9 8 7 6 5 4 3 2 1

To Nastassia

For teaching me so much more than pretty.

CHAPTER 1

The water's on. That means she's in the bathroom.

At night, this is the game we play. I win when I hear her turn the water off, then take the five steps to her door, then the three to her bed. She wins if she doesn't.

Off, then five, then three.

Off, then five, then three.

But she's still in there. She's knocked some lotion bottles off the back of the toilet and cursed. I yell in to her, "Janet, do you need help?"

"No! Go to bed," she yells back and keeps talking to herself, probably about me, but I don't care. I'm just waiting for the steps.

Off, then five, then three.

I used to think that this was crazy, having to wait like this for your mother to go to bed. But Janet isn't like other mothers. So this is the game we play, every night, waiting to see who gets to breathe first. I'm not trying to say I don't breathe during the day—I would, like, die—but breathing at the end of the night, when Janet has turned off the water and taken the five steps and then the three, and I've heard the squish sound of her mattress, is something very different.

If I win, everything stops. I can stop my mind from racing through all the day's stuff that's happened with school and friends and her stuff and everything else that scrolls down in a long list in my head, every day. But only if I win.

Only after the water's off.

Off, then five, then three.

I keep repeating it over and over, hoping that almost by magic, it will get her to do it. And then she turns the water off. And the light. Janet closes the door and takes the five steps to her door. She waits a second, then turns the knob and one . . . two . . . three . . . mattress drop. She's gone. She's out. I've won.

And I breathe. The lists of my day float by again.

First, the morning getting ready alone and sneaking out without waking her but still checking that she's in bed and that the bed is dry.

Then school and the walk with Ducks and everything he has to say. It's always a lot. And school and tests and classes and homework and Allegra and boys, which seem like a lot of trouble over not a lot of anything else.

The walk home, with the slow steps I don't even count until I open the door and find out what's waiting for me behind it. Nothing will matter much until that.

The minute I walk in the door, everything revolves around

Janet, whether she realizes it or not. Even if I'm doing homework or watching TV or texting with Allegra or Ellen or whoever. I'm never not watching her. I'm counting. Counting how many drinks she's had. Counting how many times she yells at the TV or trips on the door ledge. Counting all the time until her steps to bed and my one long breath. Counting to five, then to three.

For the longest time, I didn't even know she drank. I thought that she was just like everyone else's mom. Everyone else's mom needed help up the stairs sometimes or slept on the bathroom floor because she couldn't make it to bed. I was sure everyone else's mom turned up the music at three in the morning and danced, and wanted you to dance, too, so pulled you out of bed even though there was school in the morning; everyone else's mom could be great like that. And everyone else's mom could get sad about something and cry and pull you close to her, asking why her husband left five years ago, then push you away, cursing at him and asking how she's ever supposed to meet someone now that she's forty-five, and thank God you don't know what any of this means, since you're only thirteen.

But that's not everyone else's mom. That's just mine.

My list is short today. My book report is half finished, and Janet's offered to read through it tomorrow or the next day. She'll feel useful, and if I write it well, she'll be proud and braggy about it. She'll grab the phone and threaten to call my teacher right now and tell her that her daughter, her genius daughter, deserves an A and probably a book contract, and if she's too stupid to see that, my mother has a Peabody Award she can kiss. I fight her for the phone during this and, once I'm able to hang it up, we laugh for a while about it. It'll be early, she'll have only had a few. Once that stops, the night can go anywhere. Janet can go in any direction. She's like a bouncing ball sometimes, and if you miss it once, it bounces under a car or up onto the roof, and everything is lost, all because you missed it just the once. This is why I have to watch her. This is why I have to count.

It's over for today. All of it.

I close my eyes and I'm out.

In the morning, I always check on her first. It's the start of my day. I tiptoe the thirteen steps to her room, squeeze my way in through the sliver opening of the door, and look in at her. I look closely to see that she's breathing, but I can usually hear her. Then I have to check if the bed is wet. Today, it's not. That's excellent. Now I can shower.

A morning like this is the best part of my day, sometimes my week. It's before I have to hold my breath with Janet, and I can just take care of me. Put myself together and get a look. My favorite mornings are when clothes are the biggest worry, at least for the moment.

I need to get my hair fixed. I should tell Janet, if she doesn't notice it first. She gets really mad if I let my hair go too long and then complains how everyone will see what a bad mother she is, and she doesn't understand why I would want to do that. She can't have that. Janet's always worried about what everyone is doing or what everyone is thinking about her. Except me.

I start thinking about my look.

This September is still too hot, so I can't wear a lot of layers yet, which is a shame because I love having a switch look halfway through the day. You can do that with a cardigan or a jacket, but in this heat, the look has to be sacrificed. I get in and out of the shower, lotion up quickly too. If my elbow gets even a little ashy, Janet is in on me again about how I'm embarrassing her.

In my room, I open the closet and start putting together my look. If anything, I know how to dress. It's probably the thing I'm best at.

Janet used to tell me you can't teach taste, and I guess you can't, but I always feel like she's taught me. Even when I was a little kid, Janet would sit me on her lap and flip through "the rags." That's what she called the fashion magazines. I think I loved being close to her and hearing the excitement in her voice when she talked about Givenchy or the new collection by Alexander McQueen. My dad was living with us then, and he would laugh at how still and serious I got when Janet dropped "the rags" on the floor and called me over. Almost like I was heading to school.

"She's the only girl in kindergarten who knows Dolce and Gabbana," my father would say.

We were happy then, together. But that was a long time ago.

Today, I'm wearing a blue low V-neck, almost arctic, from Old Navy. It's not fancy, but it does the trick with this flowy navy skirt with the smallest dots of the blue in the flowers, which pop when put with this top. The skirt *is* fancy, my dad sent it from Milan with a note that said lots of things that meant make sure you call me and thank me so I won't be disappointed in you, and you're welcome for the skirt.

I put it with plain white sneakers and a very low sock, a long chain with a peacock feather on the end that I got from Ducks, and white lace Madonna gloves. I know it might seem like a lot for a Tuesday in the eighth grade, but I like it, and I need it. I always need a little something extra. It makes me feel like me, at least for a while.

I go down to the kitchen, skipping the creaky step just in case, and pour myself some orange juice and start looking for a bagel. I hate when Janet buys onion bagels because she never eats them, but she leaves them at the bottom of the bag, so they stink up everything else. Blueberries and onions don't mix anywhere. It's like how I think of Janet in general. It should be a sweet thing, living alone with my mom, Janet, the beautiful fashion writer, but there's something off. There's one onion bagel in the bag, and it stinks up everything else. Lucky for me, today there's a sesame right on top and strawberry jelly in the fridge, so I guess it's not all bad.

I grab my phone as I put the plate in the sink and see the three texts from Allegra already. Two *Hi* ones and one picture of her outfit.

It's funny because she thinks she's killing it, wearing the best outfit EVAH, and she needs to show me because I will absolutely die. I really hate to be this mean about my friend, but she never has an outfit that is the Best Evah.

She wears expensive things all the time, and I guess that's cool. But that's also her big mistake. You can shop your money away on a few expensive things, but that's just one side of fashion. There's nothing extra. There's nothing you. You will be the picture that is set out by the designer or the store. But when you go all over, and you buy cheap stuff and fun stuff and crazy stuff and pricey stuff, you get all the extra, you get all of you. You need things that mean something to you, things that tell your story. Janet wrote that once. It was a big article for her. It's her philosophy of fashion.

I guess it's mine, too, now.

I never tell Allegra what I think about her outfits. I just send her emojis that I guess she reads as happy. It makes me feel better than lying. Stupid doodles can mean whatever you want.

I slip my phone in my pocket and, with my books and folder in my hands and my pencil behind my ear, which will look old-school to highlight the gloves, I head outside to meet Ducks. He'll notice the gloves and my necklace, I know. He always does. Sometimes I do the extra just for him.

I close the door quietly. When I open it again, who knows what I'll find.

CHAPTER 2

Outside, Ducks is waiting for me by the gate. His real name is Davis, but I've always called him Ducks. He has one earbud in. He likes to do this, pretend like he's so focused on you, but there's always opera blasting in his other ear. It doesn't really bother me, but I wish he would just be honest and comfortable about it, instead of pretending that he's listening with his whole head.

"Those gloves are amazing," Ducks says as I walk down to him. "And the necklace." Then his face turns a little panicked. "Did you do all the reading for social studies?" he asks me.

"It wasn't that much," I say. My phone buzzes in my pocket with a text from Allegra, asking if I want her to pick me up in her car. That's how rich she is: Her parents have a car and drive her to school, while the rest of almost everyone we know walks or takes the train.

"Who's that?" Ducks asks.

"Allegra," I tell him. "She's asking if we need a ride." As soon as I get the words out, his panic about the twelve pages we had to read on the invention of cuneiform turns into something worse. Allegra has been mentioned. Now everything matters. Everything is a deal, big or little. It was just a car ride. I was stupid to mention it.

"No, I'll walk. It's okay if you want to go though," he says, backing away.

It's not okay at all, in fact. It's totally the opposite. It's always like this with Ducks, everything you do has a reaction or a moment when he has to wonder if he can or you can or what anyone will think or what he even thinks about it. It's exhausting for us both. What is wrong with a ride to school?

I text Allegra no. I'm walking with Ducks. I push open the iron gate and follow him down the street. When I catch up to him, he smiles. Sometimes I wish he could feel just one thing instead of twenty. There's only so much I can take before school and before Janet.

The walk down 7th Avenue is mostly quiet. The low static of Ducks's music follows us along, to remind us that we are not talking. But that's fine.

Ducks knows me but doesn't know about Janet. I know it's very strange to say, but I used to get mad at him for not knowing. I mean, every little face I make or word I say is a huge deal to him, so why can't he see something so obvious like that when it's going on all the time?

But how would he see? I cover for her all the time, and she doesn't go out enough. And when she does, she's always friendly and fun. I notice the little stuff because I have to. I look for clues to how many drinks she's had. And sometimes I want to tell him, but I know that it's easier just to keep quiet. Sometimes quiet is good.

Ducks turns to me and asks, "So you really did all the reading for social studies?"

"Yes," I answer. "How many pages did you get through?"

"Like, five. Is that bad?" he asks, scrunching his nose at me. He wants me to tell him no and all the stuff he needs to know so he can feel fine about not doing his homework. And he knows I'll do it. That's why he scrunches his nose at me. Ducks is my best friend, and even now, the minute before I dive into a full book report on the last seven pages of our homework he didn't read, I take a second to laugh at his nose and roll my eyes, because I know he knows I'll help him. It's what we do.

By the time we're out of the numbered streets, Ducks is all caught up on the beginning of civilization, and we can talk about other things.

"Well I think, I mean, really, I think Ryan *like* likes you," Ducks says, staring at the sun and not at me.

"He's never said anything," I answer.

Ryan is a friend who sometimes comes over with Allegra and his friend Brian. He's all right. He's cute, I guess, I mean, if you like boys like that. Ryan is a boy. There's no other way to describe him. He does boy things and says boy things. It's not like Boy is a separate language or anything, it's just that I don't know how I'm supposed to respond in Girl with so much Boy coming at me all the time. Lots of other girls like him, though. Emily Winter writes his name all over her homework and downloads all the pictures from his Facebook. Let her talk Boy to him.

"I mean, he is Ryan Julesning, he's a Thing," Ducks says, like it's something everybody knows and yet I need to be reminded about. Ryan is popular. Everybody knows him, and people talk about what he does. He's Ryan. Of Ryan and Brian. And Ryan of the basketball team. And Ryan with the great hair and the really sweet smile. It might also be that he's tall. He's like the Bank Tower with the big red clock near our school. A landmark or something you can see from anywhere in our classroom.

"Yeah, and I'm Sophie LeClerq. Aren't I a Thing?" I smile at Ducks. He smiles back, beaming.

On the corner of President Street, there's this cute little vintage store called Shelley's that always has the best stuff in the window, so of course I always have to stop. I love places like this, and Park Slope has a lot; vintage shops for clothes and furniture and interesting stuff that's old and you can't find anywhere else. Today in the window, they have this old mannequin with a crack in its face, wearing a cape. It's plaid, with big sections of bright mustard. The cape is loud and it would be a lot to wear every day, because it's so bright, but for a once-a-week jacket, maybe to wear every other Friday, just to change up the look on the walk to school when it really gets cold in a few more weeks, it might be perfect. This is what I'm talking about. This is the extra.

"Do you like that?" Ducks says, making a face that says he doesn't.

"Oh, come on. It's great. It'd be awesome with a hat and maybe gloves," I answer.

"I bet it's really expensive. Nothing in Shelley's is ever cheap."

"Yeah, 'cause you are paying for how special it is," I shoot back. "I mean, where are you ever going to find something like that?"

"Is special what you want?" Ducks asks.

"Sometimes. Not every day. But sometimes," I answer.

"It must be nice," Ducks says. I know what he's thinking about, but I don't dare bring it up. I don't want to get into a whole debate before school.

A few months ago, Ducks started saying I was pretty. Not in a creepy way or anything like that, not in a *he likes me* way. He totally doesn't. We're not like that at all. Where a boy like Ryan is all boy, from his sneakers to his endless supply of snot, Ducks is something else. He's quieter. He gets hurt more easily, and I don't think I have ever seen him blow his nose more than three times.

The trouble with the Pretty thing is the way he says it. It's not, like, just a factual thing like my name or my address or the color of my skirt. It's more than that. A couple months ago, our friend Ellen told him something about adjectives. That you, like, get one word and you're stuck with it. It sounds so stupid. But also, really, who cares? If you don't even get a say in what your adjective is or even get to pick the people who decide it, what's the point? Ducks worries about stuff like this all the time. So does Ellen. I would, too, but it's not as important to me. They would say that's because I got a good one, so everything is easy and fun for me.

But, Pretty, what does that even mean? It's not like *elegant* or *striking* or *beautiful*. It's just cute. Flowers are pretty. I need something extra.

I guess I'm cute. I mean, I think I can look cute, real cute. Especially when the look comes together and all the little things, like the Madonna gloves this morning, match up and tell a story. When the story I tell is mine and no one else's, when that happens, I feel great. I feel better than pretty, I feel gorgeous.

At the front of the school, Ellen is waiting for us.

"Hey," she says. Ellen always wears the same things. Once she gets into something, she sticks with it, until she's totally bored or it's falling apart. Ellen doesn't care. It's been overalls with big sweatshirts over the straps for a while now. Swimming in these clothes makes her head look really small, but I don't say anything about it.

"Nice gloves." Ellen smirks.

"Oh, I know. They're great." I smirk right back. Ellen does this thing to me almost every morning. She almost tries to make fun of me, but it's not totally like that. It's like she's testing me. If I can stand up to Ellen, I'm able to stand up to anyone else. It's her way with me, and I sort of love her for it.

Ellen and Ducks start to walk into the school, but I drag behind them, looking for Allegra. She would have waited for me. So I text her.

> Where are you?

Allegra types back:

> Just pulling around the block, stopped for Starbucks. See what you missed?

This is so stupid, it makes me laugh. She stopped for Starbucks! Allegra is crazy! Ducks sees me not walking in and stares at me. I can feel his eyes on me before I even look up from my phone.

"Do you want us to wait for you?" Ducks asks.

"No, I'm waiting for Allegra," I say, looking back down at my phone before I can see his face, which I know will be disappointed and upset. Ellen just laughs and pulls him through the double doors. She can take care of him now.

The first bell rings before Allegra shows up. Her mother drives her to school most days. It's like she read a book somewhere on what a perfect mom is supposed to be and she's just following the instructions. You don't know if she actually likes it or not. I think that's why Allegra is so mean to her. I hope it is, because if not, Allegra is just plain awful.

"Whaa-aaatttt?" Allegra says, getting out of the car.

"Allegra, please. Don't ruin such a nice morning. I'm trying to make sure you have everything you need for Hebrew school," Allegra's mom says.

"I dooo-ooah." Allegra stamps like a little girl as I walk over to the car.

"Hi, Mrs. Bernstein." I crouch down and wave to her.

Before her mom can answer, Allegra slams the car door right in her face.

She walks through the double doors as the second bell rings, never once turning to see if I'm behind her. She knows I will be.

It's already starting to be an interesting day.

CHAPTER 3

Allegra takes her time getting to homeroom, but Allegra takes her time getting anywhere. She thinks it is actually "her time," as though it doesn't belong to anyone else. She walks to her locker like nothing is going on around her, like no one is racing to get to their classrooms, like Ducks isn't waiting in the doorway of Mrs. Alexander's room, worried I might be late, but also hoping I won't see him. She walks like she hasn't already been warned twice this week about being late. Allegra walks as if none of that matters. Because to her, it doesn't.

It may sound weird, but this is the reason I like Allegra best. Nothing fazes her, and she expects nothing ever will. She's sort of "over it" at thirteen, and that feels so cool to me. It must be nice to be over it. Instead of deep in it.

"Leg, we need to go," I say, looking around as the teachers round up the last of the stragglers in the hallway. Mr. Wendell is coming toward us, but Allegra's looking at herself in her little locker mirror and talking at me about her plans for lunch.

"Don't you ladies have somewhere to be?" Mr. Wendell calls.

I turn and smile, trying to at least acknowledge him, but Allegra just keeps talking and picking out her books, one at a time, as if she has never seen them before. I can hear everyone in all the classrooms start to settle in. I try pulling at Allegra's sleeve, but she looks at me and says, "Wha?"

"Leg, c'mon, we have to get to homeroom. We'll get marked late," I say, listening to Mr. Wendell's shoes knocking against the floor a few feet away from us.

"They can't. We're here," Allegra says, and closes her locker. She walks past me and right into our homeroom like everything is absolutely right on schedule. I wave at Mr. Wendell with a smile and follow Allegra into homeroom, right in time for everyone to sit down at their desks for attendance. For a minute I really didn't think I would make it, and even as I sit at my desk, I keep worrying about what would happen if I hadn't. How much trouble I would be in for being late. It takes me a while to stop my head from spinning at the thought of what would happen if the thing I was worried about actually had happened. Allegra never thinks like this. She's over it. She's lucky for that.

First period is math, which is fine, I guess. I like math in that it all makes some sort of sense. It's not like English, where you get asked what you think something means in a story or a poem. How do you ever know? I mean, the truth is, in those olden times some guy could have been drunk and just wrote things that he thought were funny, and now there's a poem that we're all sitting around trying to figure out its meaning, who knows what, but we're supposed to know. Drunk people say stupid things, things they don't mean, all the time. It's even stupider to try to figure them out. Math is much better.

Ducks, Ellen, Allegra, and I all have third-period social studies together. I don't mind social studies. It's stories about people and cultures and history, which are mostly interesting. But then there's Mr. Gennetti. He's our new teacher this year. He's young. He just finished college, and this is his first year teaching. He's super excited about it. You can tell from the way he dresses. He has really great shoes and his clothes are colorful but not in a, like, *trying too hard* sort of way. He's got style. And he's super cute. Ellen thinks so. Allegra thinks so. Most of the girls in our class think so.

Mr. Gennetti sits on the side of his desk and starts talking to the class.

"Well, kids, how are we today?" He always calls us "kids," which should sound really awful and maybe a little babyish but out of him seems okay.

"Good," we all answer.

"Well, I'm glad to hear it. Did you all do the reading last night?" We all nod at him, even Ducks.

"So let's talk about the early days of civilization," Mr. Gennetti starts.

I'm interested because it is interesting, but what's a lot more interesting is watching all the girls react to Mr. Gennetti. They smile at him. They laugh at his jokes. They're focused on him, listening to every word, and treating him better than any other teacher in our grade. And why? Mr. Gennetti is cute.

Maybe this is what Ducks means about being pretty. Maybe it does mean things are easier, but things don't seem easier for me.

Gym is dodgeball, which I love. I think it's hilarious, and I know I shouldn't, but seriously, seeing Sara Dubwicz get hit with a ball is the funniest thing in the world. It's why I never aim for her. I'd rather watch somebody else do it.

By the time the bell rings at the end of the day, I have about three hours of homework, six texts from Allegra about going for pizza after school with Ryan and Brian, and Ducks standing by my locker door waiting to walk me home. Things are about to get hard again.

CHAPTER 4

"How was your day?" Ducks asks me as I walk over to my locker.

"Fine. It's not really over yet."

"I just meant your day at school," he says back, like he thinks I think he's dumb, which I don't.

"Allegra wants us to go with her and the boys to Pizza Plus," I say, opening my locker and not looking at Ducks's face, because I don't want to see it. He made this huge deal about my birthday and best friends and all that right before we went back to school. He thought Allegra was stealing me away from him, which is just a stupid thing to even think. People can't be stolen, but he made this huge deal about it for weeks without ever really asking me why I didn't want a big party or anything. I probably wouldn't have told him even if he had asked. I didn't want a party because I didn't want Janet to ruin it.

"I don't really have any extra money," Ducks says with a sigh in his voice.

"What did you do with your money today?" I ask him.

"I'm buying a record," he says, smiling and probably hoping I will ask him about it. But I don't. "And besides, I don't need the pizza anyway."

Ducks always complains about being bigger than he should be. He thinks he's fat, but he looks fine. It's his whole problem, he thinks, but I could tell him some other ones. One problem would be moping at my locker when he wants to hang out with me.

I close my locker and move down the hall to meet Allegra. Ducks follows me out, sulking the whole way.

When I get to Allegra, she starts telling me everything about her day, even the stuff I was there for. She talks about it all like it's some thrilling adventure that happens only to her. But it's just a normal day.

"I mean, Ms. Kirkpatrick should stop wearing plaid if she's going to talk like that," Allegra says, not looking over her shoulder at me. We're in our usual triangle, walking down 7th Avenue. Allegra walks in front, and then me a little behind her and to the side. Ducks is behind me but farther over, almost right behind Allegra, I think so he can shoot her dirty looks without her seeing. He doesn't know that even if she saw them, she wouldn't care or think they were even about her.

Ryan and Brian run in front of us, joking around in that loud-and-pushing Boy way. Ryan keeps looking back at me, though, and smiling. Maybe he does like me.

On our walk to Pizza Plus, I say about twelve to fifteen words to Allegra, she's doing all the talking. Ducks has said nothing, and now both earbuds are in. Allegra's told me about Gina Broccoti in civics, who keeps picking her nose and thinks no one notices, and about the homework she has to do, and about Ryan. Allegra really wants me to like Ryan, mostly because she likes Brian and she thinks getting one means the other will follow. But Brian isn't even nice to her. He comes over to her house to watch movies and stuff, but I think that's it. He never smiles at her. He doesn't really seem to even notice her.

Ryan opens the door to Pizza Plus for us because at least he's nice. Going to Pizza Plus is this cool thing about being older: getting to go out on your own and pick what you're going to eat and talk to all your friends. It's like for an afternoon the whole world gets taken over by us, and we can do whatever we want. How could you walk away from that? But Ducks wants to, I can see it on his face.

"I think I might just walk and get my record," Ducks whispers in my ear.

"Are you sure?" I ask him over my shoulder.

"Yeah," Ducks says, backing out the door.

"Are you not coming?" Allegra asks, noticing Ducks move out the door.

"No, it's fine. I'll see you tomorrow," Ducks says, opening the door as other kids pour in. Allegra scrunches her nose about Ducks leaving but then starts right in again about something funny that happened to her in gym, which I was there for and laughed at, at the time. But I'm expected to laugh all over again.

Brian grabs us all a table or says he does, but he just wants to sit down, while Ryan and I wait for the pizza and sodas. Allegra sits down with Brian, who mumbles a few things to her that make her laugh her loudest and fakest laugh. Allegra never orders anything because she can't have gluten, which she tells us every time. Ryan carries over the sodas and places them on the table, while I carry over the slices, pretending to almost drop them, which makes everyone except Allegra lunge forward to save me. Brian laughs, which makes Allegra annoyed at the joke.

"That wasn't funny," Allegra says, looking at her phone.

"Sorry, Leg." Allegra smiles at this, but I don't know why.

I like coming to Pizza Plus. They're my last moments before I have to head home and be alone with Janet. We never really stay that long. The boys wolf down their pizza and barely come up for air. Allegra gets on her phone, as though she hasn't been able to use it all day. I just pick at a slice and wait for one of the boys to talk to me with his mouth full.

Ryan sees me pulling apart the crust of my slice and asks, "Don't you want it?"

"Yeah, I just like to take my time," I say back. Ryan gets a little nervous at this and swallows his mouthful of cheese in one big gulp.

"How did you do on the test in Mrs. Carpetti's?" Ryan asks.

"Oh, good. I like that stuff," I answer.

"I hate it." Ryan smiles at me. "Only because I'm not, like, as smart as you."

"I'm not, like, *smart* smart," I answer.

"Sophie is, like, a sick genius, it's insane," Allegra says, not even looking up from her phone. I'm not. Not even in the, like, smallest way, but I get good grades.

"Maybe you could, like, help me study for the next one?" Ryan asks.

"Sure," I say back.

Brian makes a big snort-laugh over his pizza and almost blows sauce out his nose, which makes us all laugh even more. Allegra laughs at him again and hands him a napkin.

I knew Ryan was going to ask me to hang out, I just wasn't expecting it to happen so easily. I thought there would be more to it, really. I mean, it took weeks to just get to this. And where am I going to teach him math? I guess I'll have to go to his house.

After we finish, the boys say they're going to walk down to 4th Avenue to a basketball court there. They ask if we want to come, but I say no, which I think makes Allegra a little angry. We leave Ryan and Brian at the corner as Allegra pulls me up 7th Avenue. She waves goodbye to Brian, who doesn't even turn around.

"So you guys are, like, totally going out now," Allegra says, beaming, as soon as the boys are down the block.

"Leg, we are not." I laugh.

"Soph! You are!" Allegra says. "He's, like, in gooey gross love with you and wants to have your babies and everything."

"Wouldn't I have to have the babies?" I laugh again.

"Oh, so you want to? I knew it. You love him right back!" Allegra smiles, looking at her phone.

"I don't. He just wants me to help him with math," I say, really close to her face to let her know how serious I am.

"Sure." Allegra smirks from her phone. "It's okay, Soph. Seriously, like, you and Ryan would be the Best Evah."

"There's no Ryan and me to be the anything evah," I say.

"Not yet." Allegra smirks again.

Allegra walks me to my corner, but I hold her there. I make her get into a cab, so there's not even a chance of her coming into my house. Luckily, the cab comes quickly, and she gets in without looking up from her phone but shouting to me, "Call me, text me, message, every five minutes. I mean it."

When I get to the front gate of my house, I can hear music. It's loud, from the back of the house, her office. Maybe she's working. Maybe she's writing a lot and busy getting ready for a deadline. If it's a deadline day, I probably won't even see her tonight. She'll lock herself in the office to keep working, and all I will have to do is wait until she stumbles to her bed. It might be an easy night. I hope so.

I take my last breath, turn the knob, and walk in.

CHAPTER 5

The minute I open the door, I know it's bad. The air's different, I can't explain it any other way. It's heavy and still, thick like no one has been here for years. Like it has been waiting for someone, and I'm afraid it's me. But I've opened the door. So I have to go in.

"Is that you?" Janet yells from the kitchen.

"Yeah," I say quietly. I can hear her whispering to herself as I answer. I can picture her making faces and getting angry at me for answering her question, madder still that I came home at all. "I'm just going up to my room," I say, hoping that if I can make it up the stairs before she says anything else, I'll be safe, but the minute I hit the first step, I hear her hurrying out to me.

"Oh, no. I'm going to have some words with you, miss," Janet says, barreling out to the hallway. She looks gone, like she's had more drinks than I can count, and there's even one still in her hand. She's still in her bathrobe and pajamas from the night before. She takes a big sip out of her coffee mug, never taking her eyes off me. "You're a spoiled little thing, you know that. Spoiled rotten."

I don't move, and I barely look at her. I'm going to let her have her say, and maybe then she'll let me go up to my room. But she's started in with *spoiled*, so I might be here for a while.

"You just do what you want around here, don't you? I asked you a question!"

"Yes," I answer, even though I don't know what she's talking about. It's better to tell her what she wants to hear, as long as it gets me upstairs.

"You're talking to me like that? I will slap the black off you, girl."

"Yes, ma'am."

"You have no respect. Not for me, certainly. Barely for yourself. Look at you." Janet says this as she walks closer to me. I don't move. "Look at this skirt. Where did you get that?"

"Papa sent it to me from Milan," I say, focusing on the steps and nothing else.

"That worthless bastard. You're just like him." Janet takes another sip before she really starts in on me. "Look at you. You think you're something, 'cause you're light skinned with your skirt from Milan."

"I have to go upstairs," I say, moving closer to the step.

"You ain't got to do nothing," Janet says, grabbing me hard by the arm and pulling me down the one step I've been able to get up. My folder, phone, and books fall from my hands, and I almost fall with them. "All you have to do is stand here and listen to me when I'm talking to you. It's you and me, we're about to have this out now. You follow?"

I need to get away from her is my only thought, and I'm looking for a way out. There's a slight chance I could sneak past her, but only if she moves a little farther to the left. It's my only shot to get away. And I need to take it soon.

"Don't you just walk around here like nothing's wrong. You act like you've got it all together, and you don't. You've got nothing without me and you never will." Janet takes another step over, circling me, and it's then I take my chance. I run up the stairs two at a time, and she grabs after me but misses. She falls on the steps, cursing and screaming up the stairs, but I don't turn back, not once. I run into my room and lock the door. Janet is screaming from the steps, using every curse she's ever thought of and warning me what's going to happen when she catches me.

I hear her scramble up after me. I stay still and keep my back against my locked door. I close my eyes and wait. Even when she starts banging on it, warning that if I don't open this door, *right now*, she's going to kill me. I keep my eyes closed, waiting for her to stop.

"I brought you into this world, and I will take you out," she screams, and pounds on the door. She pounds for a long time. I never move. I never even open my eyes. She goes back downstairs, muttering to herself angrily again, she falls down the last few and must have spilled. She curses loudly and throws the mug against the front door. I hear it smash. Then she gets up and goes to the kitchen, I'm guessing to get another drink.

I'm safe, at least for now. I open my eyes and look around my room. She's already been in here and torn everything apart. Every one of my drawers is dumped out. She's ripped most of the pictures off the wall that I'd cut from "the rags," even the picture of her in *Harper's* last year. This isn't the worst, but it's bad.

There was the time she busted the tires on my bike because I was "ungrateful." Or the time she smeared makeup all over my walls because of the way I dress. Or the time she hit me so hard, you could see the outline of her fingers on my cheek for a week, because I came home late from Ducks's house.

She slams around for the first hour, but by the second she's having an argument with herself or me or whoever else she imagines in the kitchen. She runs to the bottom of the stairs to yell up to me. "You hear me, I'm not doing that!" and "Nobody can take that away from me. Not you and certainly not him." That bit is, I'm guessing, about my father, but I have no idea what any of it means. I try not to listen, because it'll only make me madder and I still have a lot to fold and put away.

I should have known when she called me "light skinned" I was really in trouble. She only gets mad at me for having lighter skin when she's really drunk and mad. It also usually means she's been drunk and mad for a while. It's not just a flash of anger that on other nights she laughs at or forgets in the next second. When she gets so mad that she hates a basic part of me, she's out for blood. The key now is to stay away until she passes out. But judging by the yelling, that won't be for a few hours.

There's nothing to eat in my room, and by seven o'clock I'm starving. My homework is on the stairs, so I won't be able to get it done until she passes out. I'm going to be up all night. I look under my bed for my laptop at least, but she's taken it. She's funny like that, she rarely breaks important or expensive things. She doesn't want to be reminded of how bad she's gotten, and the cost of a new laptop or a phone would be a big reminder. I'm alone in my room. It's getting dark and there's nothing to do but sit here and wait.

For some reason, I don't turn on my lights. I don't want to draw any attention to my door. I don't want to get her up here again, slamming and cursing at me.

I lie on my bed for a long time, thinking about all the things downstairs that will have to get cleaned up tomorrow. All the tears and apologies she'll make to me if she remembers, and the laughs if she doesn't. The garbage bags full of paper and glass that have to be taken out in the morning. My homework will have to wait until then, I guess.

She yells and bashes around until almost ten. By eleven she starts to get tired. By one o'clock, the house is still. I'm tired and almost falling asleep myself, but I open the door slowly to see if I can hear anything. Music still plays from her office, but it has been on all night. I look down the stairs and see my books and phone still there. She hasn't touched them. I take the first step out of my room, trying not to make any noise, then another, and then another. I go down the steps slowly and pick up my papers without a sound. Still I have to check on the rest of the house.

I go down the stairs, making sure to skip the creaky stair and to step over the broken mug near the front door. The broom is in the corner. She must have stopped halfway through cleaning or forgotten about it altogether. All the lights are still on. And something is smoking in the kitchen. I run as quietly and as quickly as I can on the hardwood floor to the tile of the kitchen to see what's going on. The kitchen is a mess, with papers and pictures all over the island. Two empty bottles of vodka sit in the middle with a third on the floor. There's smoke coming from the stove, so I slide over to see what she's done. She was trying to make hard-boiled eggs, I guess, but she forgot about them and left them boiling. Now all the water is boiled away, and the eggs are black and crackling. The pot is ruined and almost burned straight through.

I turn off the burner and grab oven mitts to take the pot off the stove and put it in the sink, but the sink is already full of all her other dirty and broken dishes. I don't know what to do. It smells horrible.

I decide to dump this in the backyard. There's nothing else to do with it, but that means I have to walk through her office, and I think she's in there. She's passed out, probably, but if she wakes up and thinks I ruined her eggs myself, she'll get crazy all over again. I just can't take any more tonight. I need to be so quiet.

I walk slowly to the door of her office and push it with my butt, until I turn around and see her. Her music is blasting, but she's out cold on the carpet, with another bottle rolled under the couch. The floor around her is littered with papers and envelopes. This is where it all started. Maybe she got something in the mail? Who knows and who cares.

I tiptoe to the back door. She's sprawled out on the carpet, her face pillowed by her arm. She'll be fine for the night, even if she throws up, which with how many empty bottles I've seen, she'll probably do.

The blackened eggs are smelling worse, so I hurry to the back door and open it with a free hand. I toss the eggs out into the yard. Something will eat them or maybe not, I just need to get rid of them before I throw up myself. It's cold outside, but it's like stepping into something special and dark, where no one can see you. It's an escape from everything inside with every light on. I look up at the sky and I can see my breath smoking out in front of me. I drop the ruined pot a little farther off from where I'm standing.

There are barely any stars in Brooklyn, the lights of the city drown them out. But tonight there are three, almost four, stars I can see. Seeing them makes me cry. Mostly because I'm tired, but also because they're there, and they see what's happened. It makes me feel a little less alone.

I go back into the house and start turning out lights. Janet hasn't moved, she's out for the night. I take my papers and phone up to my room. I brush my teeth and go to the bathroom—I've been holding it in for hours. In the mirror, I see how tired I am. I look how I feel. I turn out the light. I'll have to be up even earlier tomorrow to do my homework.

I go to my room and lock my door, just in case.

CHAPTER 6

I only sleep a few hours before my phone starts buzzing to wake me up. I have to do my homework. I race through a lot of it, skimming over paragraphs and filling in guesses for answers, hoping I'll have time later to check them. It's going to be a very long day.

I go out of my room slowly. Usually after a night like that, she's sorry, or at least pretend-sorry, so she's good for a couple weeks. It's why I don't clean up after her. If she has to clean up her mess, she feels worse and that puts her on her best behavior for even longer.

Her music is still playing, but besides that, there's no other sound in the house. I go to brush my teeth but try not to look in the mirror. From the bathroom window, I can hear the faint sound of bottles rattling outside on the street. It's Wednesday, and I totally forgot to leave bottles out for Jen and her grandma.

I spit out my toothpaste and run down the stairs, being careful I don't step on pieces of the broken mug from last night. I slide out to the kitchen to grab the two trash bags full of glass bottles I've put away for Jen under the sink. It saves Jen's grandmother's time, and it means she doesn't have to be embarrassed anymore. Or at least anymore today.

The bags clink with the glass inside them. So I hold them tighter at the top, hoping that the harder I hold, the less they will be able to move. I sneak to the front door, with the bottles rattling as little as I can manage. At the door, I have to free up a hand, so I set down the bottles slowly, but I hear Jen's grandmother getting closer outside, and I don't want to miss them. I open the door, pick up the bag again, allowing for a little more noise this time, and rush out.

As I step out the front door, Jen and her grandmother are right next door. Jen's grandmother gets up every Wednesday morning and takes her shopping cart, stolen from a grocery store, collecting glass and plastic bottles out of people's recyclables. She takes them back to a grocery store and recycles them for money. She never returns the cart.

The first day I saw them, I had thought Jen's grandmother was just a crazy homeless lady, but when I saw Jen behind her, carrying her schoolbooks, looking just like me, awkward and shy and clean behind her, I hadn't known what to think. So I'd asked.

"Hey . . . hi," I'd said, leaning down from the steps where I was sitting. Janet had been slamming around, looking for her wallet she'd dropped under the couch the night before. She was going to Paris, so I had to go out and keep the cab waiting for her. Jen didn't look up at me that day. Her grandmother had made these strange smiles as she nodded at me, opening my gate and going right over to my garbage. Jen had stood by the gate, looking at her grandmother impatiently and with embarrassment. The car had come for Janet, but by then Jen and her grandma were three houses away.

From that morning on, I started putting out the bottles for Jen's grandmother, to save Jen one embarrassment on the block. With how Janet drinks, there's always a lot of bottles.

I barrel down the stairs carrying the two big bags of clattering bottles, and Jen's grandmother almost claps, she's so excited to see them. Jen sort of smiles, but her embarrassment never really goes away. I don't want her to feel like that, especially with me, but I understand. I pass the bottles to Jen's grandmother, who bows and smiles. Jen's grandmother says something in Chinese to Jen, who thanks me for the bottles.

"It's okay. I never mind doing it," I say as Jen's grandmother moves on to the next house. I step through the gate and follow Jen onto the street.

"Do you have parties at your house or something?" Jen asks.

I laugh, but Jen doesn't.

"Oh, no, my mother is a drunk," I blurt out, still laughing by myself.

Jen smiles a little but doesn't know what to say, and neither do I, so I keep laughing. I can't believe I said that. I've never told anyone that. Never said anything close to it. I couldn't. It's different with Jen today.

All Jen says is, "I'm sorry. Are you okay?"

For some reason, I keep laughing. "Rough night." And then I look into her eyes and say, hoping she'll believe me, "I'll be fine." I usually walk Jen to the corner, but this morning I make an excuse and go back to my house. It was easy to tell Jen the truth, but it's hard to live with having told her. I still have to get ready for school.

When I get back in the house, Janet's awake. She's walking around the hallway looking at everything she's done and probably remembering none of it. I can see it on her face before she realizes I'm there. As I close the door behind me, she looks over at me.

"What went on here?" she asks me.

"You don't remember?" I ask.

"No," she says, looking at me, then at the broken mug on the floor.

"Yeah," I say. I half want to lie, but I half want to tell her the whole truth, down to every nasty thing she said and how I had to hide in my room. But for now, *yeah* is enough. She starts to cry. She rubs the heels of her hands into her eyes. She puts her hand out to me, and without even thinking, I shiver and move to the side. Her eyes widen, like she can't believe it. I expect her to get angry, but all she can do right now is cry.

"Oh, baby," she says through her hands covering her mouth. She's crying all alone. Just like I was last night.

"I have to get to school," I say, and walk up the stairs. When I get to the top landing, I look back and see her sitting on the steps, her head hanging between her shoulders. She's still for a minute, but then her back starts to shake.

By third period I'm exhausted, so I ask to go to the bathroom to splash water on my face. After the third splash, Ellen comes out from one of the stalls. She's looking down at the floor. Then she looks up, sees me. I watch her compose her face into a look that is completely innocent but it's totally a lie.

We're both hiding out in the bathroom.

"Sick?" Ellen asks.

"I'm tired. I didn't sleep," I answer, drying my face. "Are you all right?"

"Yeah. Why?" Ellen asks, getting a little rough. But then she seems to decide, and this part I can see her think right in front of me, that I will catch her if she gets too angry, so she stops. "I just needed a break from class. I'm not into it today."

I laugh a little. "Me neither."

"Why didn't you sleep?" Ellen asks, looking at me through the mirror.

There's a lump in my throat, and I know if I swallow or open my mouth in any way I will burst into tears. I just look at her in the mirror and splash more water on my face so she won't be able to tell if I start to tear up even a little. Everything is right on the edge, so I don't say anything.

Ellen waits for something, but she knows me better than that. She puts her hand on my back and says, "Only four more periods, then we're out." Ellen leaves me right after that. She's a good friend.

After school, I'm supposed to hang out at Allegra's house, but I ask if I can just get a ride home. I'm not feeling great. In the car on the way to my house, she keeps talking about nothing, and I'm listening a little, but mostly I'm just trying to stay awake.

"Am I, like, boring you?" Allegra asks.

"No, why?" I say, opening my eyes, which I am sure isn't helping my case.

"Are you sick?" Allegra asks, looking at me for a second before she goes back to her phone.

"No. I'm just tired. I didn't sleep," I say, getting quieter with each word because I don't want Allegra to ask why I didn't sleep. Though she probably won't anyway.

"Were you worried about Ryan? Jeez, I didn't think you liked him that much," Allegra says loudly, smirking to herself.

"Sure," I say. I'm bobbing my head off the window near my seat, just wanting to get closer and closer to my house, which gets me closer and closer to my bed and farther and farther away from Allegra.

"See? I, like, knew it. And he's totally into you. Like, it's a little weird, not that, like, liking you is weird, don't think that. It's just, like, that he's, like, so out about liking you. He smiles at you and follows you around, always says nice stuff to you. It's, like, romance or something." Allegra smiles.

There's something in the smile that I can see even with my eyes almost shut. She's listing all the things Ryan does to me and wishes Brian would do them to her. And then she gets mad.

She looks at me like I've stolen something.

"It's nice, but it's not, like, anything serious," I say back.

"It could be though. He really likes you," Allegra says. She gives me that look again.

"Yeah, but I don't even know if I like him. I mean, he's nice and, like, cute or whatever."

"He's seriously cute. Kate Brenman is heartbroken that he likes you so much. She's had a crush on him forever, and he barely even remembers her name," Allegra says, getting a little more upset.

"Well, that's not my fault. I'm not in charge of Ryan," I say back, getting annoyed. I'm not doing anything. I don't even know if I like Ryan, and if I do, so what? Allegra is looking at me like I'm taking something, and I don't even know if I want it. She wants hand-holding and making out, and she's not getting any of it. She thinks I am or am about to, or she thinks I am throwing it away.

"Well, if you don't like him, you should at least tell him," Allegra fires back at me.

"I didn't say that. I just don't know. It's a lot, you know?" I say. I know this whole conversation has much more to do with her and me than either of those boys, so I add, "And really, I'm just taking my time, Leg. I mean, I sort of have to hold out for Mr. Gennetti, don't I?"

This gets a laugh.

"OMG, he's the sexiest thing Evah! It's not fair. But you seriously need to figure things out with Ryan," Allegra says. I don't know who she's talking about. Not fair to Ryan or not fair to her?

"I will. I promise," I say as the car turns onto my street. "This is me," I say to the driver. "Thanks for the ride, Leg."

"Sure. But, like, go to bed. You need to sleep. You look bad," Allegra says as I close the door. This is probably the clearest conversation we've ever had, where we actually talked about what we wanted to talk about or were at least honest.

I get nervous when I go through the gate, but mostly I'm thinking about my bed. The rest I can deal with.

Probably.

CHAPTER 7

Opening the door, I hear Janet talking to someone. She sounds so small. I don't think I've ever heard her voice sound like that. Then she stops, and the other person stops too.

"Hey, Sophie, is that you?" Janet yells from the kitchen.

"Yes," I say now that I'm caught. Even an apology will take hours of talking and promises to get better, which will never actually happen, and all I want to do is sleep. This could be worse because she's brought someone else in to embarrass us both. She's never done that before.

"Sophie, baby, don't keep me waiting now," the other person yells out to me, and suddenly everything changes. It's my auntie Amara. With her here, things won't get out of control. She's too bossy and funny to ever allow any of that.

I run out to the kitchen and see my auntie Amara standing near the island. Her grayish dreads are perfectly spun around in a head scarf that matches her dress with just two or three strands hanging over one side of her face to balance her out. She always has a great look. She holds her big hands out to me with all her ringed fingers spread as wide as they can go just to catch all of me all at once. I run up and hug her as hard as I can. Her boobs are so big, they almost smother me as she pulls me closer and closer to her. It feels like the best way to be crushed.

"Oh, baby, you feel good against my heart," Auntie Amara says, and I can feel each word tingling against my face.

"When did you get here?" I ask, finding some air, but not pulling away.

"This afternoon," she says as she lets me go. "Now let me get a good look at you. Girl, you grown! And look at this face." Amara takes my face in her warm hands and squeezes the bottom of my chin.

"Janet, why didn't you tell me you had Dorothy Dandridge living in this house with you? You get that face from me, you know."

I look over at my mother, who seems small and nervous, almost sick-looking alongside Amara. But I think she'd look that way on her own. Maybe it's because she's so skinny and slight in comparison to Amara, like someone with a terrible disease, but she just smiles at me, or tries to.

"Now you run upstairs to get washed up for dinner. And we'll talk about that hair later," she calls after me.

I don't remember going up the stairs. That's how tired I am.

I sit down on my bed for a minute and wake up an hour later to the smell of Chinese food. From my room, I hear Auntie and Janet talking, the sounds of their voices but not their actual words. Janet sounds whispery and scared, almost like she's hissing, and Auntie sounds loud and firm, clucking back at her. Even though I don't hear the words, I know they're talking about me, but I can't hear enough to know if it's good or bad.

I rush down the stairs just as Auntie calls me to come down for dinner. I walk so fast, I almost trip over the suitcase in the hallway.

"Going somewhere?" I ask Auntie.

"Actually, your mama is taking a trip," Auntie Amara says, walking with me to the kitchen. Janet is sitting in there, with her same cup of coffee.

"I have to head to Paris for a month," Janet says, just looking at her cup. "It's for work. A big story. I need to see a bunch of shows."

Janet says this like it's the worst thing that has ever happened to anyone in the world, but I don't know why. She loves Paris, she jumps at any chance to go. Paris is her favorite place. It's where she met my father. She has lots of friends there. So what is her problem? When she does look at me, her big eyes are almost full of tears.

"And I'm going to stay here with you. How do you feel about that?" Auntie smiles. She's setting the table, like she's already moved in and taken charge.

"Fine," I say, looking at Janet. What is she doing? What is this about?

"Just fine? Girl, I expected a better answer than that. I never get to see you, and now we get a whole month together, and you're 'fine'? Just 'fine.'"

I don't take my eyes off Janet. I keep looking at her, trying to figure out what is going on with her. Why is she acting like this? Does Auntie know about last night? Does she know about any of it? Am I supposed to tell her? And what is Janet going to do on her own in Paris? What is she thinking; a week is one thing, sure, but a month? She can't keep it together for a month and certainly not a month in Paris.

But Auntie pushes in. "We're going to have a good time, you and me. Your mama and I figured that it would be easier for you if I came than to have you up to Harlem with me." Amara teaches college at CUNY in the city. She's really smart and a little famous to certain people.

"When do you leave?" I ask Janet, who stares at her coffee.

Janet gets up from the table, pretending to look at the Chinese food. "Tomorrow morning. Car's coming at six."

"And when do you get back?" I ask, looking at her harder and harder, trying to get her to look back at me.

"Not now, girl, rice's getting cold," Auntie interjects, pulling out a chair for me to sit.

Everything is so formal tonight. We're all putting on a show of how things are supposed to be but never are. It annoys me. Janet and

I never sit at the table. It's usually too covered with papers or mail. We eat in our rooms or at the island, watching the news or *Jeopardy!* We barely use plates, let alone silverware. There's a whole drawer full of plastic stuff that comes every time we order in, which is all we really do. I'm surprised to see we have metal forks at all.

But I'm hungry, and I'm not going to start with Auntie Amara, not now.

Janet sits down in the side seat, looking at the egg rolls and the dishes but never at me, and never at Auntie. They ordered cashew chicken, which is my favorite, but with everything else going on here, I'm not even excited about it. I reach in to scoop some onto my plate, but Auntie stops me.

"I'll serve. Hold on a minute." Auntie smiles, swatting me to sit down. She makes up a plate for Janet and then for me. It's one weird thing after another.

After I swallow my first mouthful, I turn to Janet.

"When do you get back?" I repeat.

Janet looks to Auntie Amara, like she's checking something. Then, looking back at her plate, she says, "In about a month, like, five weeks, probably."

"That isn't too long to put up with me, is it?" Auntie Amara asks loudly, trying to pull me closer to her, but I don't move.

"When were you going to tell me, Janet?" I say, getting a little more angry. She's abandoning me.

"Oh, now, that's your mama, girl," Auntie Amara says to me. Janet still doesn't turn around.

"It's my name," Janet says to her coffee cup. "I have to go, Sophie, and I have to go tomorrow. I'm sorry."

"There's nothing to be sorry about," Auntie Amara interjects. "We'll be fine, won't we, Sophie?"

I take a big, angry bite of a crunchy noodle.

"Yeah. We'll be fine," I say really loudly so Janet can hear me. We'll be fine without you. Probably better. It's you who should worry. You're the drunk.

"Yes. And it's *Auntie* to you. We're friends, but I'm your aunt before that. You get me?" Auntie Amara smiles at me.

"Yes, Auntie." I smile back.

We eat so much of the Chinese food, except for Janet, who stares sadly at her plate and picks at the rice, sipping her coffee, which has to be cold by now.

It makes me mad that she doesn't say anything. She explains nothing to Auntie. She just sits there and pretends like this is the way we operate every day.

When we're done, Auntie tells me to help her get all the dishes. Janet sits quietly. I take her plate, which is still filled with rice and broccoli she's pulled apart.

"Are you finished?" I ask her. Now I'm not looking at her. *Let's see how she likes it.*

And then she looks up, and with the saddest eyes I've ever seen says, "Yes. Thank you, Sophie." I can't help but look back at her. I'm angry with her but her eyes look so sad, it's hard to stay mad for too long, so I look away. I take the plates in to Auntie, who is washing everything in the sink, even though we have a dishwasher. She says she does a better job.

"What do you have for homework?" Auntie asks me. I know it's not a big question, but it's one I haven't had to answer in years. I can't remember really ever having to answer it. Janet never asks, and even if I ever have a big project, I am always the one to tell her. Why does Amara need to know about my homework anyway?

I ramble off the list of things I have to do tonight. Mostly worksheets and reading, stuff I can get done on my own in my room, no big deal. Auntie nods after each item and asks a question about the subject and what the teacher expects from me.

"Well, that sounds like a lot. Bring it down to the table here while I clean." Auntie Amara smiles.

"I can do it on my own," I respond.

"I know. But I would rather see you do your work in case you have a question or something. Then I can check it over when you're done."

Okay, what? Not only do I have to report in, but now I have to do my homework in front of her and she is going to correct it when I'm done? That's crazy. Why would she do that? I mean, I know she's a college professor or whatever, but I know how to do my homework. I do it all the time and I don't need any help. Why can't I just be left on my own?

I don't say any of this, though, and I bring down my books and sit at the island as Auntie Amara cleans, not just the dishes but the stove and the refrigerator and every flat surface in the kitchen.

When I finish the last of it, I close my books and start putting papers back in my folder, but Auntie stops me.

"Oh, no. Let me see." Auntie smiles. She peels off her yellow gloves.

"You were serious?" I answer.

"When I'm joking, you'll know, little miss. Now show me." Auntie laughs.

I take everything out all over again and try to get her through it as quickly as I can, but Auntie keeps slowing me down over and over again. Looking at every question and answer, even correcting my work. I don't get why she has to do this and wonder if it's going to be like this every night for the next month while she's here.

"And what's this?" Auntie says, holding up my social studies book.

"Social studies. We're learning about Mesopotamia," I answer.

"What about it?" Auntie smiles.

"Just that it's the beginning of civilization," I answer.

"Oh, no, it's not. It's one part of it, but humans started their history in Africa. Your teacher tell you that?" Auntie smiles up at me as she flicks through my book.

"No. Mr. Gennetti said this is where humanity started," I answer.

"Well, tomorrow tell Mr. Gennetti he's wrong. Or I can." Auntie laughs out loud. "I'm teasing you, but know that Mesopotamia is only part of the story. Now run upstairs and brush those teeth. I'll come up and kiss you good night."

The whole time I'm working, Janet's been sitting at her computer, frozen so still I'd swear she's a statue. It's like she's already left.

Upstairs, I pace in my room for a bit. What is this? I mean, it's not even 9:00 p.m. and I'm getting ready for bed? Who's going to watch Janet and turn out all the lights and make sure the stove is off? Who is going to count her steps from the bathroom to her bed, to make sure that she gets there at all?

Auntie knocks at my door. "Baby, can I come in?" she says as she's already through the door. She sits on my bed looking around my room. She sees the ripped-up magazine pages in the garbage from the night before. "I'll bring you up a garbage bag for this."

Auntie pats the space next to her on my bed and waves me over.

"You and me, we're going to do all right, aren't we?"

"Sure," I answer, sitting next to her and getting pulled over by her thick arm.

"This is a big opportunity for your mama, and she needs to take it seriously."

"Okay," I answer.

"So I need you to be good for me. Okay?" Auntie asks me.

"Yes, Auntie, I will," I answer. It all still seems like so much pretending, and I don't know when it's going to end. Auntie holds me close for a minute and then kisses me on the forehead. "I'll be up for breakfast, all right?"

"All right." I don't know what else to say. Everything is about to change, and I can't figure out what it's all going to change into.

Auntie stands at the door watching me get into bed. I feel like I'm doing this just for her. She turns out the light and closes my door. My room is so dark, but I want to stay up, I need to stay up and count the steps. Auntie doesn't know anything about our house or what goes on here. What if something happens? Tonight nothing was like it regularly is, who knows what comes next? I'm so tired in the dark that as hard as I fight, I can't keep my eyes open, and the next time I open them, it's morning.

I hear the front door open, so I jump out of bed and head to the front window to look out to the street. Janet has her coat on, and Auntie puts two suitcases into the trunk of the black cab. Davis's mom is there too, holding Janet's hand. They hug hard, whispering into each other's necks—at least that's what it looks like from up here. Auntie comes up behind them and tells Janet to get into the car. Janet looks up at the house, and for one second I think she sees me looking down at her. She looks away, and the cab door closes. Auntie and Davis's mom wave to the car as it drives away and then head back to their houses. Coming up the stairs to the front door, Auntie sees me in the upstairs window and waves.

When she gets inside, she yells up, "Sophie, how about some eggs?"

Eggs? It's too early for hot food. What is she thinking? But I just yell down, "Fine." Things are only going to get weirder from here on in.

CHAPTER 8

Returning from school is so different for those first few days. One day I come home and the whole house just smells like spices. There's steam on the windows and on the pictures in the hallway, and loud music playing from the kitchen. I stop pretty quickly after hearing it and then, without thinking, run into the kitchen. Even though I know Janet's not home, and I know she would never be cooking, let alone cooking something this good, the steam and the music make me think she's done something wrong and she's too drunk to know any better and I need to fix it before it gets out of hand.

In the kitchen, Auntie Amara is swaying to music, slow and sexy-like. She still thinks she's alone, she's dancing for herself. But then she turns, sees me, and keeps moving in the slow-swaying way anyway.

"How're you doing, baby?" She doesn't care that I'm here. She doesn't even care that she can't really hum. She's just doing whatever she wants, however she wants to do it, including cooking whatever she's cooking in my house and steaming the whole place up.

"What are you making?"

"Oh, I am cooking up something special for you and me tonight. You ready? You ready for something good?" Auntie says this as she dances over to me, dipping and diving at me. I don't want to laugh, but I can't help it. Why does she have to dance like that? Why does she have to dance at all?

"Go on and wash up and come right back down to help me." Auntie smiles as she sprinkles a bright yellow powder into a boiling pot. From the minute I walk in the door to the minute I leave in the morning, she's always ordering me around and telling me what to do. I'm still not used to it.

I drop my books on my bed and head to the bathroom. My look today is good, very good in fact. Fall is my favorite part of the year, especially in Brooklyn, and layering is my thing. Today, I have this off-white blouse with a dark green cardigan with little Scottie dogs all over it. This with a skinny stonewash and pink high-tops is a look that I love. It can be anything, and even though I try never to repeat, at least exactly, I am seriously thinking about keeping this as an ensemble for a while.

Ducks loved it. Especially the high-tops.

Auntie Amara calls up from the kitchen, "Sophie, come down when you're ready. I'm serving this all in the living room."

Okay, now what exactly is she thinking? We don't eat in the living room. We never have because of the white carpet. Janet never even allows drinks in there, and it's the one rule that she actually follows. Usually we don't even turn the lights on. But now I guess with Auntie here, none of that seems to matter. There are no rules anymore. Auntie's in charge, and the rest of us, meaning me, just have to get used to it.

In the living room, Auntie's set up on pillows on the floor. She's taken pillows from almost every room of the house. She's also lit every candle in the house, even ones that are just for show.

"Honey!" Auntie yells up to me as she walks in the room with a big bowl in her hands. She doesn't even see me standing there. "You coming down? Oh, you're right here. Well, sit." She puts the big bowl in the middle of the glass coffee table. It's like a salad, almost, but there's hot chicken in it and avocado. I don't know what it is, really, and I'm not sure I want to.

"I want to do something nice for you, baby. You deserve it," Auntie Amara says as she rubs my shoulder. What does she know about what I deserve? She doesn't know what goes on here. She doesn't know what it's like. She's just here because I think it would be illegal to leave me alone, even though I would know how to take care of myself a whole lot better by myself and there wouldn't be dirty dishes in the sink.

"Do you want a napkin?" Auntie asks, handing me one. "I should get some towels or something to put underneath us, I guess. I don't want to get anything on the rug." She sits down on the floor.

Then why are we in here? If you are so worried about getting something on the rug anyway, why are we sitting on the floor and eating some sort of hot summer salad? None of it makes any sense.

"I'll get them," I say, getting up and walking into the kitchen.

"Thanks, baby, and would you bring me that bottle of wine on the counter?" Auntie yells as I pass her and start into the kitchen. *So now she's drinking?* I lost one drunk and replaced her with another. The kitchen is a mess, oil splotches all over the stove, at least fifteen different bowls all filthy and gross piled up in the sink. Knives out all over the counter. It looks worse than when Janet was here, and still there's music on. I go over to her computer and hit the space bar to pause it so I can think straight through all the mess.

"Aww, why did you turn that off?" Auntie yells from the living room.

I walk over and hit the space bar again, grabbing two towels from the drawer and the bottle of wine she's already started before going back into the living room.

As soon as I get back: "What's wrong, don't you like Miss Patti?" Auntie laughs.

"I'm sorry. Here's your towel," I say, handing her the towel and the bottle.

"How was school?" she asks.

"It was fine," I answer, taking my first bite. It's actually kind of good.

"You don't say much, do you?" Auntie smiles. "I understand. I want you to know that I'm here for you." I can feel her eyes on the top of my head, as I'm bent over my plate trying just to eat and get out of here. "Look up at me," she says loudly. So I do, but why does she have to tell me even where to look? "Sophie, baby, I'm here for you. I don't need you to hide from me, or hold anything back from me. Do you know that?" she asks.

"Sure." I barely get that out with my mouth so full.

The song changes on her computer, and Auntie waves her hand, in excitement, I guess, and just like that her glass of wine topples over and spills on the white carpet. Auntie frowns a little and starts to the kitchen. But I'm already up and back with paper towels. I knew this was going to happen. Why did she have to bring us in here? Why does everything have to change?

Auntie comes back into the doorway while I'm patting the wine out of the white carpet.

"Leave it. I got it." Auntie comes behind me and moves my arms away. She has a big canister of salt and a bottle of seltzer. She pours it on the spot. She's just making it worse. She doesn't know what she's doing. I can't believe she did this. I can't believe I let her. I should have stood up to her. I should have told her we don't eat in here. Janet will be so angry, and I know I will have to pay for it, of course I'll have to, because Amara won't be here and it will be just another thing that Janet can throw a drunken fit about.

But just like that, the wine starts to come up.

"I told you I got this." Auntie smiles from the carpet.

I can't believe she did it. I stare at the spot, trying to see the stain, but it's gone.

"It's only a rug, girl. There are more important things." Auntie smiles. "Now, you were telling me about school?"

CHAPTER 9

The next day at school, Allegra waits for me by the door after English. "Hey, how was it?" she asks.

"Homework, but whatevs. How was yours?" I ask her, dipping my head a little to see if I can at least trap her eyes in a look, but she's already moved to the hallway.

"Mr. Gennetti is giving us a big, like, project or whatever for after Halloween. It's, like, almost too much."

"What is it?" I ask.

"He'll tell you. But don't, like, worry or anything. It'll be easy for you. Like everything else," she says, passing into her next classroom. This is about something else. Allegra usually acts weird, but she's even weirder than her regular *I don't care* weirdness.

"Save you a seat at lunch," I call out after her.

Maybe I'll find out at lunch.

I rush into Mr. Gennetti's class right after the bell rings and take my seat in the front. Before I sit, I see Ducks looking for me, making a face, like he's not happy about my being late. Ellen is in her seat behind me, but she's not looking up at me or at anyone else. What is wrong with everyone today, and why do I have to worry about any of it?

"So as you all know, Halloween is coming up. Right?" Mr. Gennetti asks the class, and we all nod yes. "But do you all know about the Day of the Dead?" There are fewer heads nodding, but that's just what he wants.

"Well, you see, in my culture, on November first we celebrate the Day of the Dead, or *Día de los Muertos*." When Mr. Gennetti says this last part in Spanish, I think Amy is going to pass out; she hangs on the roll of his *r* like he's sending it just to her. I turn around to see if Ellen notices, because this would be something that she'd love to see, but she's still not looking up. I nudge her desk a little and she looks up. I stick my tongue out at her, which at least makes her smile after she sticks her tongue back out at me.

"On this day, we celebrate and remember the members of our families who have died."

"My grandmother died last year," Kara Geller says out loud, smiling like she finally has something to say. Too bad her grandmother had to die to give her this chance.

"I'm sorry to hear that, Kara." Mr. Gennetti smiles at her. That reminds Kara she should be sad about it too. Kara frowns it all up like she's sad all over again, if she ever really was.

"But this is a day to celebrate the dead and to keep a small part of them with us. Now, I know you all want to be zombies for Halloween, but I'd like to ask you this: If you could dress up as a member of your family, someone whom you are proud of, someone who inspires you, who would that be?"

The girls in the class almost start to hum about whom they would dress up as, but also for the chance to impress Mr. Gennetti with his own project.

"Over the next month, I want you to do some research. Talk to your parents, your grandparents, your aunts and uncles, and find out about your family. And for the Day of the Dead, I want you to write a report on the family member who makes you the proudest."

Emma's hand shoots up. "Do they have to be dead?"

"No, I guess not, but it is the Day of the Dead," Mr. Gennetti says, shrugging. "You'll present your work to the class, and I would love if you could dress up as them." Mr. Gennetti smiles really big at this part, which makes most of the girls in the class nod along, and even a few boys. Ducks does. I'm already thinking, *I have no idea what to do or who to be.*

At lunch Allegra tells me the boys want to take us to Pizza Plus again. I can see Ducks shrink at the thought. He doesn't want to go, and honestly neither do I. I tell Allegra I can't, which sets her eyes rolling so far back in her head she looks possessed, and Ducks shares a shy but sort of thankful smile over his chocolate milk.

Ducks finds me after the last bell of the day and starts to walk home with me. He's quiet, mostly, which for some reason doesn't feel heavy like usual. It's not the silence of not knowing what to say or being nervous at what you might; it's a silence between people who don't need to say much because they already know. We're just there together, and that's enough. I never really know how it works, but with Ducks, I love moments like this.

About halfway home, Ducks says, "You could have walked home with Ryan. I wouldn't mind."

"Thanks, but I wasn't going to," I say.

"I thought you guys, like, liked each other?" Ducks stares at me.

"Maybe?" I answer, because really, at this moment, *maybe* is the best answer I can come up with.

"Okay." Ducks smiles.

"I'm not trying to be weird about it, but with Ryan, like, honestly, he's fine. But who needs all that?" I smile back.

"All what?" Ducks asks, laughing.

"He's, like, a jock and he does that thing with his nose." I laugh back.

"Yeah, but that's just boy stuff. Boys are like that."

"You're not," I answer.

"No, but I don't want to be. That makes most of the difference," Ducks answers. "So what are you going to do about it? About Ryan?"

"I don't know. I have lots of other things to worry about," I say.

"Like what?" Ducks asks.

I want to tell him everything but instead I change the subject. "I mean, what about that project for Mr. Gennetti? So much work, and I don't even know who I would be. I mean, I don't know most of my family."

"That's not true." Ducks smiles.

But it is. You don't have family around when your mom drinks like Janet drinks or works like Janet works. So it's just us, and now Auntie.

"It's just a project, it's not that huge," Ducks says.

"You can't do it the night before," I say back, knowing that's exactly what he will do.

"I'm not going to, I already know who I want to be," Ducks says, louder than he needs to. He'll be his grandfather Jock. Jock died a couple of years ago, and Ducks was the saddest I have ever seen anyone be about anything. He misses him all the time. Jock was a nice man. Ducks was lucky to have him.

I walk Ducks to his gate, and right before he leaves, he turns around and hugs me. We just walked home together, what's the big deal? But it's still nice to have a hug from my friend. Maybe I needed it more than I knew.

I open the door to my house, and out of habit, I stop and wait, tiptoeing to the stairs, thinking I need to get up there before she catches me at the door. I make it up at least five steps when Auntie

Amara calls to me from the kitchen.

"Hey, girl, how was your day?" I stop on the stairs, because I don't know what to do.

"Fine," I yell back.

"Come down, if you want to talk to me," Auntie yells back.

"I need to go to the bathroom," I say as I race up the steps. Maybe I need to run away from her too. Why does she have to be after me all the time, and why is she spending so much time in the kitchen anyway? I drop my stuff on my bed and just stand in the middle of my room for a minute.

"Sophie, girl, come down," Auntie Amara yells up.

I smack my head, I'm so mad. Why can't she just leave me alone? I stamp around and make screaming faces that I know she can't see but I don't care if she does. I slam around my room until I go back down the stairs.

The kitchen is full of Auntie smells, her food and her incense, which she lights all over the house just like the candles. Even her music fills the room, and it's so loud I can barely hear what she says.

"I'm making gumbo," Auntie says, without looking at me. "You should wash up and bring your homework down here. I'd like the company."

"I can't do my work down here. It's too loud and there's no room for me. I have a desk upstairs."

"Use the desk in the office." Auntie smiles, tasting the gumbo.

"I'm not allowed," I say.

"I allow you, Sophie," Auntie says, putting the big spoon back in the pot.

"I don't want to," I say louder. Why can't she just let me be for a minute?

"That way if you have questions, I can be right here."

"I can do my own homework," I say to her.

"You best watch that mouth when you're talking to me," Auntie says, still smiling. It's a warning to me, and I should take it, but I just want to go upstairs.

"This is going to take another forty-five minutes. Go upstairs and do your work, but you bring it down when you're done, and I'll check it."

"Fine," I say back, huffing out the word like she's being ridiculous, which she is.

"Yes, it is. Now go on." Auntie smirks as she waves me out of the kitchen.

I run up the stairs two at a time, just to get away from her, and slam my door. I slam it so hard, it's the only sound in the house. I want everything to stop for a minute but it just doesn't. It never does.

CHAPTER 10

Allegra asks me to sleep over Friday night. When I ask Auntie if it's okay, she asks why I can't have Allegra to our house. First off, it's not "our" house, it's Janet's and mine, and secondly, I don't have anyone over if I can help it and especially not to sleep over. I pout around until Auntie says I can go, but I have to be home early Saturday so we can get my hair done.

Friday at school, Allegra can't stop talking about all the fun stuff we're going to do tonight. She's almost trying to impress me, making sure I will definitely show up. She doesn't need to, I really want a night away from "our" house.

"Tonight is going to be the Best Evah!" she squeals at the end of the day as she pulls me by the arm, out the door, down the stairs, and onto the street, where we get into a car and squeal off to her house and all that fun. For most of the car ride she doesn't even look at her phone, which for her must be torture. She just grins at me as we race to our sleepover.

"Tonight, I was thinking, like, face masks and old movies. Then we can order, like, food or whatever and talk to the boys. It's going to be super rad."

"Whatever you want to do," I say, trying to be as excited as she is, but I don't think without a six-pack of Coke I can be.

Allegra's house is very nice, very fancy and very modern, but it doesn't really feel like a house where people live. It looks too much like a catalog to think people actually sleep and go to the bathroom here. But they do, all the Bernsteins, Allegra and her mom and dad and her older sister, Kylie. Kylie and Allegra hate each other, and they remind each other daily. And when company is over, it only gets louder. They like to glom onto the new person to prove they're right about how awful the other one is.

Kylie is in high school and she's a super cool girl, like Allegra is or will probably grow up to be. They're really the same person. Maybe that's why they can't just get along or make it through dinner without throwing something. Kylie likes me though. She always says nice things about my clothes, but she uses her compliments to me as a way to make fun of Allegra. Kylie has a good look, except for all the lip gloss.

When we walk into Allegra's house, her dad is rushing out to a big lawyer dinner and passes us in the doorway with a "hello" and "order whatever you want," his card is on the counter. It's all in a flash and then he's gone. I think we might be alone in the house. We head to the kitchen to get Vitaminwaters. That's one of the interesting things in Allegra's house, there's never a big container of anything. They don't even buy milk by the gallon. It's all little individual bottles. Vitaminwaters and Snapples and bottled water. It's all there so everyone can have their own, because in this house, nobody shares.

"What do you want to do first?" Allegra asks, passing me a water.

"I don't care. I'm fine," I say.

"Well, do you want a snack or something at least? I think there's, like, fruit and stuff around, we don't have to order the food yet."

"Yeah, that's fine. I'm fine," I answer.

Allegra's already started looking at her phone. It's not because I'm boring her, she'll do this all night, even when it's just the two of us. It's her thing, I don't get offended by it. I just wish I knew what she was actually doing on there. I know she's not texting because she doesn't have that many people to text anyway. There are maybe five people she texts regularly and I'm one of them, and I'm sitting right here.

"We should, like, absolutely have the boys over. That would be cool, right?" Allegra asks.

"Leg, I don't want them to come over," I say.

"Why? Did something, like, happen with Ryan?" Allegra asks, looking up from her phone.

"No, I just thought it was going to be us tonight."

"It is us, but it can be us and them," Allegra snaps back. She turns to the refrigerator and pushes her glass under the ice maker. "Well, I already invited them, so if you don't want them to come, you should text and tell them not to."

"Leg, why did you ask me if you already asked them?" I shout over the sound of the ice tumbling into her glass.

Once the ice is done she turns and gives me the worst look, with, "Because I didn't think you were going to, like, freak out about it."

We order the pizza after we scroll through a bunch of YouTube videos on her flat-screen TV. It's fun, mostly, but I'm always thinking about the door and whether it's the boys or pepperoni. When there's a knock on the door, Allegra runs to get it, and from the way her voice changes, I know it's the boys, not the pizza.

Allegra is beaming when she brings them into the front room. Brian, without saying hello, flops down on the couch like he lives here, while Ryan comes over and sits with me on the floor.

"We ordered pizza, it should be here, like, any minute," Allegra says loudly, trying to be a good host. Brian sort of nods and mumbles out a "s'cool," while Ryan starts to talk to me.

"Hey, what are you guys watching?" Ryan asks.

"Just, like, random stuff." I've been trying to get Allegra to watch the new fashion show from Givenchy, but she's more interested in making fun of people in makeup tutorials or cat videos. I think it's also because it's twenty-two minutes and we both know she can't sit still for that long.

"Have you seen the guy on the trampoline?" Ryan asks.

Brian perks up from the couch and says his first full words in the house. "Oh yeah, sweet." He takes the remote out of my hand and starts to type the word *trampoline* into the search bar, and from the thousands of videos that come up, he scrolls until he finds a specific one.

It's a compilation of videos of people being idiots on trampolines, none of it goes well. One girl tries to do a backflip and falls face-first into the metal rim. A couple of boys jump so hard that they get thrown off, one through a bush. I see why it's funny, but I wouldn't ever just look this up. It's funny when the people in the video get up and laugh about it. It's funny if you know they're okay, but when one fat guy jumps on with a bottle and rolls around in pain because he knocks his front teeth out, that's sort of gross. I am the only one who thinks so. The boys scream with laughter, Brian even does an impression of the guy, he's watched it so many times. Because Brian laughs, Allegra laughs harder, and louder, than both of them to show how cool and likeable she is.

Ryan sees me not laughing and stops. "It's funny though."

"Sure, I guess," I say back.

"Next one you pick, all right?" Ryan smiles as Brian calls him to look, dude, look, as a kid flips onto the roof of his garage. The boys keep watching and hitting each other, and when the pizza shows up, I go and help Allegra grab it. There are two big pies, because she knew the boys would be hungry and she knows that Brian only likes pepperoni, so he practically gets his own pie. Allegra will grab a slice, but she'll just end up picking the pepperoni off and eating that. Pepperoni doesn't have gluten. Pizza was a dumb thing for her to order in her own house.

"Are you still mad they came?" Allegra whispers to me when we get to the kitchen.

"Leg. I wasn't mad," I answer loudly.

"You seemed mad," Allegra says, getting plates.

"I wasn't." I take two plates. Allegra takes two plates, and I know it's not a big deal, but I almost get a little mad, because I know she's going to take a slice for Brian, and I guess I'm expected to take one for Ryan. He can get his own pizza, I don't need to do that because, what, I'm a girl? I leave the other plate on the counter and go back with just my plate.

"There's pizza," I say as soon as we get back in the room. Ryan smiles and gets up and runs to the kitchen. He would have brought me a slice, but I get mad at the thought that I have to do it. Allegra puts a plate down in front of Brian as he types in with the remote, *Grill fails*. Now we're going to watch people set themselves on fire and laugh, or at least they will.

For the next hour, we watch people fall, girlfriends get pranked all sorts of ways by their awful boyfriends. One guy even tricks his wife into thinking that their son fell down a flight of stairs. Some of it is funny, but after a while you think people have to be the stupidest things that have ever lived and are probably still stupider for filming how stupid they are.

I laugh on and off, but I'm bored. I look at my phone a bunch and start texting with Ellen.

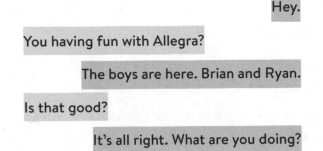

Hey.

You having fun with Allegra?

The boys are here. Brian and Ryan.

Is that good?

It's all right. What are you doing?

Ellen sends me a GIF of a cat stuck in the toilet, and for the first time all night, I laugh at something funny. Allegra glares at me and says loudly, "Sophie, put down your phone for, like, a minute, okay?"

She just said that to me. Allegra, whose eyes I didn't even know were green until we hung out for three months, just told me, in front of these boys, that I'm on my phone too much. Is she joking? 'Cause she has to be joking. Almost out of, like, shock, I stick my tongue out at her.

She wants to say something, something mean, but just as she's about to, the front door opens and it's Kylie, which is bad news for Allegra. She's caught, she's about to be embarrassed big-time and she knows it. I would usually feel sorry for her, but tonight, I'm just looking at my phone. Kylie walks into the living room, taking her earbuds out, the music still blasting from the dangling bud.

"Where's Mom, Spaz?" Kylie asks. "Spaz" is Allegra.

"I don't know. Get out," Allegra yells.

"Does she know you have boys over?" Kylie yells back.

"Yes, and she's fine with it," Allegra shouts, getting really furious.

"Fine, I'll text her and ask," Kylie says, walking out of the room and putting her one earbud back in her ear. Allegra gets up and chases her into the kitchen. We can hear them scream, but I'm the only one who laughs. Brian and Ryan look worried. Well, Ryan does, Brian is quiet now but in a different way. He stared at Kylie the minute she came into the room, or mostly Kylie's boobs.

Allegra comes back into the living room, totally distraught, almost like she's going to cry. "Sorry, guys, my sister is being a total bitch!" Allegra yells just so Kylie can hear it in the kitchen. "And she says you guys have to go."

Ryan smiles and says it's cool. Brian doesn't say anything but just gets up and goes to the door. Allegra keeps apologizing, but neither really seem to care. Ryan smiles at me, so I smile back and walk them to the door. Allegra walks Brian out, but he barely looks at her and goes to grab his bike. Allegra rushes back to the kitchen to argue with Kylie. I'm left at the door with Ryan.

"Hey, can we walk home on Monday?" Ryan asks me.

"Sure," I answer.

"But, like, just you and me," Ryan says.

"Yeah," I say. I don't know what this means, but why not? I mean, it's just walking home, right? It's not a big deal, and I do like him as a person. Maybe I could like him as more.

Ryan smiles a big smile as I close the door. For the rest of the night Allegra talks about everything Brian did, making half of it up or reading into the rest. Each and every thing is talked about as a clue to see if he really likes Allegra or not. I want to say yes because I know how much Allegra wants a yes. But the only thing I know for sure is that Brian likes to see people fall. I don't tell Allegra about Ryan walking me home Monday, I know it would just make her mad, even though it's not a big deal to me.

To her it would be the Biggest Evah.

CHAPTER 11

When I get home the next morning, Auntie is already up and in the kitchen.

"Morning, baby," Auntie says, smiling as she comes into the hallway. "Did they feed you breakfast?"

"No," I say, looking tired and hoping that she'll just let me go upstairs, but she won't.

"Well, you need to start the day off, don't you? You and I have lots to do. We need to get that hair taken care." And with that, she walks back into the kitchen. She doesn't tell me I need to follow her, but it's implied.

"How was your sleepover?" Auntie asks me as the frying pan sizzles.

"Good. I don't know," I answer, not even really paying attention.

"Well, who does know, Miss Sophie? Get a plate," Auntie says, scrambling the eggs in the pan. Always another order. I get up, grab a plate from the cabinet, and walk over to her at the stove. She scoops the eggs onto the plate and puts salt and pepper on them, right in front of me without even asking.

"There's ketchup on the counter." She smiles at me, which is my signal, I guess, to sit down and eat. "This was Allegra's house you were at last night?" Auntie asks me.

"Yup," I say.

"What's Allegra's story?" Auntie continues.

"I don't know," I say, not even looking at her now but keeping my eyes mostly on the eggs.

"You are just a font of answers this morning, aren't you?" Auntie laughs to herself.

What does she even want me to say? Why does she care about Allegra or what her story is? "Allegra is my friend," I answer, huffing a little as I do.

"A good friend? How come you never bring her around?"

I don't answer that one, because I don't know how. So I stuff my mouth with eggs.

"How are the eggs?" Auntie smiles. I nod and stuff my mouth full again.

"My mama used to make us wonderful eggs and bacon, keeping the grease for weeks and weeks in a big jar on the counter."

"That's gross." I laugh.

"It's the furthest thing from gross, girl. It's insurance. You use that grease, you can guarantee everything you cook is going to be good. Your mama doesn't cook for you that much, does she?"

"No. She's busy."

"Sure." Auntie smiles like she means more than just that word. "I love to cook, but I love to eat even more, as you can see." Auntie laughs hard at this, but not as loud as before. "You and your mama got all the skinny, and my mama and I got all the rest. But I don't get any complaints about it." She laughs again. "Your mama ever talk to you about your grandmama?"

"No, Janet never tells me anything," I say.

"Our mama was hard on us. Lord, hard as nails," Auntie Amara starts. "Worse on Janet than me 'cause Janet was so pretty. Like you. She had to do well in school, bring home straight A's, go to college, God help her, and she had to stay far away from boys, or there was hell to pay." Auntie laughs. "And those boys! They followed her around in swarms, with my mama always waiting at home to swat them away. Sometimes with a broom." Auntie Amara laughs again. "And there was nothing to do about it. We had to be good girls, had to be the first in our family to go to college, both of us being something, making something of ourselves." I finish my eggs quietly and don't tell Auntie Amara about the boys coming to the sleepover. I don't need her getting out the broom.

"Finish up your eggs. We need to get this hair done. Today." Auntie smiles as she walks out of the room.

Auntie and I ride the subway to the downtown part of Brooklyn.

I don't usually come here and I'm glad about it. It's dirty down here and crowded with people rushing in and out of these shops that you've never heard of but that sell everything from jeans to vacuum cleaners. I really wish I knew where she was taking me.

Auntie keeps stopping wherever and whenever she wants. We're obviously not in a hurry, like everybody else. She stops at a man's card table and buys some incense. He's selling these bright-colored plastic bracelets that would go great with jeans or even a button-down, but I don't dare ask for them. I don't know where we are or where we're headed, so I just stay close to Auntie Amara and watch. She stops to look at poster of a gray-haired man. "Oh, Billy Ocean, I should get tickets to that. Do you know him?"

I just look at her, because I don't and I don't really know how she would expect me to. She smiles and takes my hand. It seems babyish, I guess, to be holding her hand, but then, I feel safe. I feel connected to her, which I guess is obvious, but it's more than that. It's happiness.

We stop in front of a little storefront with floor-to-ceiling glass windows. There are posters of smiling girls with great hair, or what I'm guessing *was* great hair; the posters look greenish from having been in the sun too long. Inside I see lots of women. It's a salon, but I've never been to a place like this before.

Auntie pushes open the door, and all the voices and music whoosh out at us in a big gust of sound that almost makes my eyes flutter. The shop is small, with only about six chairs, but each is full, with more women waiting in chairs scattered around the place. A young girl in a really booby shirt comes over to the little desk at the front and looks at her book, then at us.

"How you doing? Do you need an appointment?" she asks.

"It should be under Watley. It's for my niece," Auntie Amara says loudly.

"Hey, baby. You ready to get done?" the young woman asks me. I have no idea what to say. "Aww, she's shy! Well, don't worry, baby. Miss Chantel gonna do you right, okay?"

"Okay," I answer softly. Auntie and the girl laugh at me, I guess they don't get a lot of shy girls in here. The girl says we can sit down in the front near the windows while we wait for Chantel.

It's not that I'm scared to be here, I'm not at all. It's just so exciting; I never get to come to places like this and it's a different world. The women in the shop talk loudly, but it never feels like shouting as much as reaching out to the person they're talking to. It seems like they all know each other. They're interested in each other and want to talk with and about each other. They seem happy, and happier still to be together, but there's also a feeling like it's a show. There are jokes and stories that are told not to one person but to the whole room. Everybody's involved, it's like being at a club, and even though we have a lot to catch up on, we're instantly part of the whole thing. Barely anyone says hello to us, but we are welcome. The older woman with her head in a towel sitting next to Auntie tells her how beautiful I am and smiles at me.

"Say thank you, Sophie." Auntie nudges me. And I do, but I'm still a little nervous. It's not nervous, it's a feeling like holding in a laugh. It tickles your throat being so close to something that you want but don't know how to finally have. These are all black women, beautiful black women, and besides my mother and now my auntie, I don't really get to be around too many. It's a strange thought that hits me as I sit there, but it's the truth. Most of my friends are white. I don't notice it all the time, but right now, as I'm sitting there clinging to my auntie, I think how out of place and yet totally at home I feel. I live in a different world, but this one seems so wonderful. Even to get my hair done, Janet takes me to a little shop in Park Slope where this white girl named Leslie, who's covered in tattoos, does my hair because she has a daughter from Malawi.

Janet wouldn't want me to come to a place like this. She'd be mad and call this some ghetto beauty shop. She'd make any excuse to stay away from here, but the biggest one would be me. "You're not like that, Sophie. You hear me?" But sitting here, I want to be. They're laughing real laughs and cursing, which makes me smile, especially as they try to correct themselves in front of me, thinking I've never heard worse.

Auntie starts a conversation with the women sitting next to her and hands me one of the magazines on the small table in front of us. I have never seen a single one of these "rags" before. They have names like *Black Hair* and *Hype Hair* and *Trendz*. They're so different than any of the "rags" in our house, and they all have black women on the cover. There's not a copy of *Vogue* or *Harper's* anywhere in here. I leaf through the first magazine, looking at all the different kinds of hair and different kinds of women.

Chantel, who's doing my hair I guess, waves me over to her chair as the woman before me gets up to let the dye set.

"Hey, baby. How you doing today?" Chantel smiles at me in the mirror.

"Good," I answer.

"She's great with one-word answers," Auntie yells over to Chantel, who laughs. I should be embarrassed but I laugh too.

"What do we want to do to this pretty little thing today?" Chantel calls to Auntie.

"Let her decide," Auntie yells back.

"Your mama's brave, girl. I still have to tell my two girls what they're doing and when, and they more grown than you. So what you want to do?" Chantel looks at me in the mirror.

"She's not my mother. She's my aunt," I say, trying to still be nice, but also correcting her, which I don't think she expects. But Chantel just smiles.

"Then you must be one very lucky girl to have so many good females in your life. So what're we doing with this hair today?"

I think of all the faces on the magazines I saw today and all the possibilities of things I want to do but probably can't. Or can I, and when I think for just a second longer of what I want to do, I blurt out only one word. "Braids. Like in this picture." I get up and go over to the table and pick up the copy of *Black Hair* I was last looking at, turning to the page with Gabrielle Union on it.

"Okay. I feel you. But that's gonna take a while. You and your auntie got the time for that?" Chantel smiles into the mirror and looks over at Auntie. Auntie nods and sees the smile on my face beam from across the room. I'm thrilled. A new look, a look I've always wanted but never had, and more time here. Hours more time here.

Chantel spins me around in the chair and says, "Well, sit tight, little miss. You about to get done."

It takes hours to get all my hair braided. It's a long and tiring process. Chantel takes breaks, but then so do I. We talk a lot. Auntie and the woman next to her, who I find out is named Nancy. She works at the hospital a couple blocks over. She's going to the Dominican Republic next week with two friends, and she wants to have her hair perfect for the trip. Kendra, the girl who checked us in, keeps offering me water or a Coke. Latrice has a little mini fridge near her chair that she always keeps fully loaded, but I'm fine. At one point, Kendra runs and gets hamburgers for everybody, because we've all been there so long. Chantel works hard on my hair, and as the braids take over my head little by little, I feel closer and closer to the room. She has a daughter my age. "Though not as sweet as you." The ladies all laugh at that. My auntie does, too, but then launches into a list of nice things about me.

"She's very independent. And smart. Sophie gets straight A's," Auntie calls out.

"Course you do, girl. What you want to do when you're grown?" Chantel asks me.

"I don't know," I answer.

"Well, you got time. And if you can't decide, you can come here and take Kendra's job. At least you'd keep that book organized!" Chantel says loudly, less to me than to Kendra. They start to bicker and fight a little, but it's all a game they play with each other. Both of them are smiling the whole time.

"All right, Sophie, girl, look," Chantel says as she turns the chair around and lets me see. I look like a completely different person, but I recognize myself. It almost seems like more of me than I'm used to. My hair is bouncy and alive, the braids tickle the back of my neck like rain. They wave and move in pieces and as a whole, and I love all of it. It's better than I could have imagined, and everything I wished it would be. It's beautiful and for the first time, I feel like I am too.

CHAPTER 12

Sunday morning I go into the bathroom and still can't believe that it's me looking back from the mirror. My new hair is so beautiful, I can't stop looking at it and swinging it around my smiling face. I stand in the bathroom for a solid fifteen minutes, just grinning at myself in the mirror, before Auntie yells up to me.

"Sophie, are you almost ready to go?" Auntie calls from the hallway.

"Go where?" I ask, stopping, a little embarrassed at what I'm doing. But I know she can't see.

"Girl, now, I told you I was taking you to church, and I meant it. I need to stop by my apartment and get my hat. It's going to take at least an hour on the train. Are you ready?"

"I can be," I yell back, almost hoping that she'll say never mind, but knowing she won't.

"Well hurry, please! I want to get to the church in time to get a good seat."

"Are there good seats in church?" I smile at myself in the mirror again, thinking she's obviously making a joke, but the look on her face when she enters the room lets me know right away that she isn't.

"You need to get ready, that's what you need to do. Questions you can save for the train. Now come on, please!" Auntie Amara says, shooing me away with her wide hands.

"I have to email my father," I say quickly, hoping that maybe this will get me out of it. But she just sighs and stops.

"I forgot. Well, make it quick so we can go," Auntie says, talking to herself on her way down the stairs to the kitchen where I can't hear her anymore. But then she turns around and yells again. "Oh, and don't mention your mama being away, all right?"

Why is she worried about this? Why would he care that Janet is in Paris? I mean, if anything, he'd probably like to be warned that she's in the same city, but he likes to fight with her just as much as she likes to fight with him, so why not tell him and not give him another reason to be disappointed in me if he finds out on his own? I want to ask Auntie about it, but I don't know if she will even tell me, so I race to my room and get on my computer.

My father lives in Paris, and I don't really see him much. We don't visit. We mostly email and Skype every couple of weeks, and my father and I play a delicate game with each other. It comes out of the fact that I don't really think we like each other much. So in every conversation we have or email we send, we both try to trick the other into something. I'm usually the one with more to do, convincing him that everything in the house is perfectly fine and that Janet is great. He usually doesn't believe it and then he goes into his things that he knows are just untrue, like how I should come and live with him or how much he misses me. Neither of us believes what the other is saying, but we are willing to go along with the lie as long as we can both feel like we tried to have a relationship with each other. We probably both have a hard time with it.

Since today is just an email, I have a much easier task. When he responds, that'll be when the real trouble starts. Auntie Amara calls up the stairs to remind me that it's getting late, so I end the email with a half-hearted mention of my class project about family. Heritage. He'll like that. He'll want to teach me some more French, which means an hour on Skype of him correcting my pronunciation and rolling his eyes at how I can't even speak the language he speaks every day.

Auntie is getting anxious downstairs, so I hurry to get a look together as quickly as I can, but I don't know what you're supposed to wear to church. I've never been. I'm guessing a dress, so I pick out a floral one with green tights. I throw on my fuzzy pink cardigan and black shoes, guessing that should be a church look, but I'm not sure. I add a few bracelets just to see some of my story and run down the stairs. My braids bounce with every step down to Auntie and make me smile all over again.

Auntie waits at the bottom of the stairs and looks at me, but she doesn't smile. I hope it's just that she's too nervous about the trains and getting a good seat to notice my outfit and doesn't just plain hate it. She rushes me out the door and straight down to the subway. It isn't almost until we cross the bridge that she says anything about it at all.

"You look good. You do well, little miss." She smiles as she picks fuzz off my shoulder. Just as we cross into Manhattan, four boys get onto our car and yell, "What time is it? It's showtime! What time is it? It's showtime." They clap along as they ask people to move away from the poles so they can dance. This happens a lot on the train, and usually I try not to pay attention, but for some reason Auntie nudges me to look, so I guess I have to.

The boys start to dance and flip on the standing poles and handrails above our heads. They're actually really great. One boy throws his legs up in the air and catches his feet on the ceiling rail. He's popping his shoulders the whole time and making his way down the aisle, fist-bumping with anyone who'll pay attention to him dangling in front of them. Auntie does, and just to please her, I do too. The boy makes a big deal of me, fanning himself and making a kissy face right at me. I turn away because I know he's kidding, but Auntie gives him a look that almost makes him fall off the rail. When each of the boys has danced, they go around and collect money, and Auntie hands them a five, still giving the upside-down boy from before a look. She smiles at me, though, so I feel fine.

Auntie Amara was right, we're on the train almost an hour.

We have to transfer to another train until we get up to 125th Street and Broadway in Harlem. It's so awful to say, but I've never been to Auntie Amara's apartment. I start to feel weird about it, I mean, we live in the same city, and getting from Brooklyn to Harlem is a super-long ordeal, but it's not impossible. It seems silly that I've never been here before.

We walk the two or so blocks to her apartment. Auntie's apartment is the complete opposite of my house in almost every single way. Janet likes everything white and spare. She likes things to be put away. Surfaces, walls, even her bed is white and empty. Auntie's apartment is stuffed to the brim with colors and pictures. Hundreds of photos, masks, beads, and all sorts of stuff cover the orange-painted walls in the hallway, and the purple ones in the living room and green ones in her bathroom. It's a full house and it feels like that even though it's been empty since she's been staying with me. I look through as many pictures as I can take in while she rushes to get her church hat from the bedroom.

"Can I borrow some of these for my class project?" I ask from the hallway.

"Sure," she says as she comes back from the bedroom, with her big swirling hat on. With one hand, she pushes me into the hallway, grabbing her pocketbook and keys and locking the door. She doesn't say anything else about it. For now, she's saving her breath, we're in a hurry to get a good seat.

Auntie walks ahead of me for the next five blocks to an old stone building. Lots of women with great big hats like hers are piling inside, so I know we're in the right place. I follow behind her until we get to the doors and an older woman stops us both to say hello.

"Well, Amara, who's this little lady with you?" the older woman says, taking my face in her hand. She's gentle, I can feel it through her hand on my face. I smile at the thought, which I guess makes it less weird to be touched by a total stranger.

"Mrs. Threadgood, this is my niece, Sophie," Auntie says, standing behind me.

"Look at this face. Pretty like this must make the Lord happy for all his good work," Mrs. Threadgood says, laughing with Auntie as if I wasn't even there. "You ready to hear the Word today, child?"

"Yes," I answer, having no idea what she is talking about. She smiles and walks with us into the church. It's already filled with people. We get seats a few rows back from the front, and while Mrs. Threadgood and Auntie talk about people they know, I look around. Unlike me, everyone seems happy to be here, but I guess it's growing on me. Church seems like a special place, and anyone who comes is special just for being there. It's hard to describe, but even though I've never been before, I start to feel part of it too.

Then the choir of about twenty-five people, all dressed in robes, comes in from the side door and stands up on the front stage. The room changes almost immediately. It's about to begin, and everyone knows to start to pay attention. A small woman holds her hands up to the choir, and they begin to sing in one big voice. Sharp, precise words that thank God for his love, and when the drums start in, and the guitar and the piano pick up, we're all involved. Everyone starts to stand and clap along. Even Auntie claps along, singing all the lyrics, which she already knows. She waves to me, telling me to clap, which I do, but by the time I catch on to the lyrics, the song is almost over. Music continues throughout the rest of the service.

Then the preacher comes out and begins to talk in a loud and raspy voice. He stops and starts in the weirdest places, but the music plays along with him and the people shout, responding to him, egging him on to say more. People in their seats call out as he speaks, agreeing with him when they do and laughing when he makes them think about something they hadn't thought of before.

"And that's the point. That's the point of it right there," he says, and starts in again. "We can't just love this part of him, or that part of her, even though that would be easier. Wouldn't it? I'd love to love just bits of you all, believe me. But my God, and my heart, ask for more than that. They ask me to take in more, to extend my hand farther out, past where it is convenient, past where it is easy, farther out not to where it is comfortable but to where it is needed. And who calls me? Who pulls me out, farther and farther and farther on? Who?" The crowd is agreeing with him louder and louder, calling him to tell us who, even though they know it too. When he finally says the name Jesus, the whole room erupts in shrieks and applause. Even Mrs. Threadgood raises her arms up and yells, "Praise Him!" to me and everyone around her. Auntie smiles at me but doesn't say anything. I think she's hoping that I'm not bored and that maybe, just maybe, I'm liking it. I smile back to let her know that I am.

When the reverend finishes he sits down, even with the crowd still yelling for him. The choir woman who conducted before gets up and introduces her granddaughter. A small girl in a pinkish dress comes out, acting more afraid than I think she's ever been in her life. She is going to sing her first solo today. Everyone in the room is waiting. It's like we all know, before she opens her mouth, that she's going to be wonderful, or at least we're all wanting her to be. I know I do.

"Precious Lord, take my hand." Even in the first phrase, her voice is perfect. People around me all start to nod, happy that they were right. Or maybe because they know her, or because they believed in her and they want everyone to know just how much. Ladies in big hats call out for her to sing. Sing! And she does, and we lean even farther forward in our seats, just trying to hear more from this voice singing for us. When she sings about being tired, weak, and worn, I hear the words for the first time, but know in my bones what they mean. I know what that feeling is, and she does too. When she asks the Lord to take her hand, I don't know why, but I start to cry. Not an ugly cry but tears that brim out of the bottom of my eyes and drip down my cheeks while I smile. It's like the tears didn't want to miss out on this moment either.

Auntie sees me and draws me close to her, patting my shoulder and rocking me to the music as the choir starts to join in behind the girl. When the song is finished, the whole congregation cheers for her in one loud voice. I'm screaming to her myself. She smiles a nervous but a happy smile, probably glad that it's over with, but I hope she knows how well she did. I want to tell her if she doesn't. I feel in a strange way very close to her now.

After the service, Auntie has coffee in the basement with all the ladies. Everyone treats her like a sister. Most of them actually call her that. I don't talk much to anyone. I'm not rude, I answer when anyone talks to me, but I keep looking for the girl who sang. I want to tell her how wonderful I thought she was while I have the chance, but she never comes down.

When it's time to go, Auntie has to say about a thousand goodbyes before we can actually leave. Walking back to her apartment, Auntie holds my hand. It's beginning to feel so right with her. We don't say much to each other, but we are fine with the silence. We stop at her apartment so Auntie can change.

"How did you like church?" she calls from the bedroom.

"It was great," I yell, looking at the beads on her wall but keeping my hands behind my back the whole time.

"I saw you catch the Spirit today." She laughs.

"I just loved that song so much. That girl."

"Oh yes," Auntie says, coming around the corner. "Her grandmother was proud of her today."

"Yeah," I say. "Do you always go?"

"As often as I can, I do," Auntie says. "I like to see folks, and the music is good."

"And God?" I say, I don't know why.

"Well, that's a different matter altogether." Auntie smiles as she enters the living room. "You want to try on those beads? You keep looking at them."

I don't know what to say. I feel caught and embarrassed. But without even stopping, Auntie walks to the wall and takes these beautiful pea green beads and puts them around my neck.

"I got those in The Gambia. They look good on you, girl," she says, turning back to the kitchen to open up some of her mail. I start asking her about Gambia. She's been so many places, some of which I've barely heard of, and she knows all these people, none of whom I know. I'm flooding her with questions but, rather than getting annoyed with me, she just answers and seems happy to do it.

"This is Sonia Sanchez, she's a poet and activist." They spoke at a conference.

"This mask came from Botswana." She went there in 1991 for the first time. She wants to go back. She has pictures of her trip somewhere in a box.

"This is Angela Davis." She's Auntie's hero and friend.

There's a small black-and-white photo of two little girls in pretty white dresses and gloves. As soon as I point to it, I know who it is, but I want to hear Auntie tell me.

"That's me and your mama, going to church." She laughs. "I hated it then. But our mama made us go every Sunday. Dressed up like dolls. On our best behavior, or else. Even God couldn't help us out of the trouble we'd be in if we embarrassed our mama at church."

I look closely at my mother's little face. She's not smiling, and you can tell she doesn't want to go, but Amara is holding her hand, like she held mine today. She seems a little happier about it. We have that in common.

"It's the thing about church. I go mostly because I know my mama would want me to. She didn't expect us to believe, and I don't think either of us ever really did." Auntie smiles at the picture and a little at me. "But going to church is part of our history, it's family without the blood but with all the rest. With all the love when it's good, and all the silliness when it's not. That's all there, too, isn't it? It makes you feel good to be part of something."

I look at my mother's small face and say yes.

Auntie Amara grabs a small bag and a photo album from her room, brushing me out into the hall as she locks the door and walks us out to the street. It's so fast, we're almost at the subway before I realize I still have the beads on. I stop cold, thinking I have to take them back right now. I'll break them or lose them or something. I panic a little bit and tell Auntie that I can run them right back, but Auntie holds my hand and pulls me toward the train. "Keep them, baby. They suit you."

CHAPTER 13

I wear Auntie's beads to school, because they go with my look, or I want them to. I want them to be part of my story. I actually design my whole look to match them. I love them so much. They're so precious. Maybe too precious. All day I worry about breaking them or losing them. Mr. Gennetti sees them during class while he's telling us all about the pyramids. He flashes a smile at me that makes Amy and Kara both cough a little because it's not them. But it does nothing for me. When school gets out, Allegra's already waiting for me by the double doors like she has something big to say to me. At least I think that's it, she's never waited like this for me.

"Are you walking home?" I say to her right away.

"No, but you are, with Ryan," Allegra says, smirking at me. Her phone is waiting in her hand, and the minute the bell rings, she turns it on.

"How did you know about that?" I say as we walk out. Ryan is already waving to me out on the street. Allegra looks up from her phone and smiles the biggest smile she can put on her face when she sees him waving at me. Brian is talking to him with a bunch of boys. Allegra watches Brian walk off but then looks back to me and *oohs*. She's back on her phone and in a cab before I can even get her to answer me.

I walk over to Ryan. He seems nervous and a little excited. *We're just walking home*. He asks which way I want to go, and I say, let's walk by the park. It's out of the way, but maybe that will get him to relax a little.

"Thanks for, like, walking with me," Ryan says.

"Sure," I say. "I'm happy to walk with you. It's not a big deal."

"I know, I'm just saying." Ryan smiles. "I really like hanging out with you."

"Thanks." That was probably the wrong thing to say, but I did mean it. I know I should be nervous or, like, fluttery about walking home with Ryan, but I just feel bad that he feels that way. I know that this is supposed to be the moment that whatever is happening between me and Ryan finally happens or at least starts to happen, but it seems like a big deal over nothing.

"I know it's, like, so weird to ask, but could I hold your hand?" Ryan mutters, not even looking at me.

"Sure," I say, and take his hand. I guess Auntie got me over this bit. I don't want him to freak out or whatever so it's just easier to do it. His hand is clammy, but I don't say anything about it because he's having a terrible time already. I thought this was supposed to be a nice thing. Holding his hand seems to calm him a little, and when we get to the park, he starts to talk. In fact, he starts to talk a lot. He's talking about school and basketball, and he's funny about them both, at least when he wants to be. He's also nice; the more he talks, the more I think that. And he's cute. Even him being nervous starts to get cute. But besides holding his hand and listening, what else am I supposed to do? Is this all there is to being a girlfriend?

When we turn the corner to my street, he gets a little jumpy again. It's almost like something is going to happen, but I'm not sure either of us knows what it is. I start to laugh a little. Maybe because I'm nervous too. When we get to my gate, he stops, still holding my hand, and says, "What are you doing Friday?"

"I don't know?" I reply, wondering what else I should say.

"Do you want to go to a movie? Like a date?" Ryan asks.

"I'll have to ask my aunt." I smile. I guess this is what he was nervous about.

"Okay," Ryan says, letting go of my hand. "I'll see you tomorrow?"

"Sure," I say. I guess I like Ryan, and if it's just holding hands, I guess it's not such a big deal. I watch him as he walks down the street. He keeps turning around and looking at me and smiling. I can't help but smile back.

The next day, Ryan waits for me and walks me home from school, holding my hand with his clammy palm. And again it's nice, and I don't mind, but he still seems so nervous. Though once we get to the park, he seems to get calm again, and when he's calm he starts to talk. He tells me a story about when he was little and his mom brought him to the park and he got lost. He ran off by himself and like five seconds later didn't know where everyone was. He was so scared. He started yelling, "Mom! Mom! Mom!" All these moms around heard him and ran over to help. He was surrounded by them, all trying to help him or get him to calm down. Finally his own mom showed up, she must have seen the commotion. She was in tears, and so were some of the other moms. It was a pretty funny moment at the end of everything. He smiles a kid's smile, like he's half embarrassed and half happy for telling me. I think of him as a little kid, small and afraid, and I don't know why, but I like him more for that.

When he leaves me at my gate, I run up the stairs, not anxious to get away from him but just to get a moment to be by myself and think about him and what this all is. It's easier to think when he's not in front of me. I like him. I think he's nice. I guess I wouldn't mind being his girlfriend. I might like it. It's exciting either way. I'm smiling about it, so that must be something good.

I smile through most of the rest of the night. Auntie notices and is happy for it. She thinks I'm always a little too serious. Maybe she's right, but I have to be. It isn't until after dinner, cleaning dishes from the living room floor with Auntie, that I remember how I haven't heard from Janet since she left. Nothing at all, actually. Usually, she would have called me by now, at least to show off being in Paris. But nothing. Not a phone call or an email or anything. Not even a text.

I think to ask Auntie about it, but I almost don't want to jinx it. I don't want to start counting the days until she gets home and it all changes back to how it was before. I'm liking so much of how it is now. Even Ryan.

"And who's this boy that keeps walking you to the gate? Don't think I don't see, little girl." She laughs.

I smile. I'm not embarrassed. I mean, I guess I am a little, but also I'm shocked that someone, someone adult, knows anything about me and wants to know more. And that she's not angry about it.

"He's cute for a white boy," Auntie says, laughing so loudly, the water ripples in my glass.

"His name is Ryan," I say. I'm nervous now and I don't know why.

"Do you like him?" Auntie says, taking my glass and putting it in the soapy water.

"I guess."

"You guess? He must be doing something wrong." Auntie smiles.

"He's nice," I answer with a little smile. I start to look up at Auntie, but she's just waiting to hear what I have to say next. The trouble is, I don't know what to say next.

"Nice? How?" Auntie asks. She's getting serious, but I don't know how to handle this. I don't know what to say to make her happy or at least to make her stop asking me any more about it.

"He walks me home," I say.

"And holds your hand."

"Yeah, but that's it. I promise," I say back loudly, trying to show her how serious I am and how serious I am taking all this. Even though I don't know what "this" even is. It's like when she spilled the wine, I start to get so nervous that I've done something that can't be fixed. I don't want her to be mad at me. Right now, if she told me I was in huge trouble, and that I could never see him again, I'd do it. I would do anything she told me to. Maybe that means I don't like Ryan as much, but maybe I don't. I can't worry about that at the moment. I can't let this new life with Auntie Amara end. I can't go back to being alone here in the house, with rooms I can't go into and things I never get to say. I can't have nights I have to lock myself in my room. I can't count the steps till she makes it into her bed. Auntie Amara sees me getting lost in all of this and touches my face with her soapy hand.

"It's okay, girl. Don't get nervous. We're just talking." Auntie hums.

"He's nice," I say back.

"You said. Can I meet him?" Auntie asks.

I have no idea how to answer. But I'm nervous so I blurt out:

"Yes."

"Good, I'd like that." Auntie smiles. "You're a pretty girl, do you know that, Sophie?"

"I guess."

"Girl, don't guess at things you know. I have seen you getting ready in the morning. Nobody who thinks they look like nothing spends that long trying to turn it into something." Auntie Amara laughs loud again. "It's a good thing."

I never think of it as a good thing or even a thing at all. I just think of it as me.

"Boys are going to be a big part of your life. They're gonna be chasing you left and right. But the thing you need to know right now, and know it for always, is: You're in charge."

"What do you mean?" I ask her, really confused. Am I still getting in trouble?

"You're a special thing in this world, baby. And you always have the right to say who you let into your life and who you don't. It's about understanding how special and worth it you are, and demanding the same from other folks."

"I don't want to be conceited," I say, scrunching my nose up and shaking my head no.

"That's not what I'm saying at all. You're a treasure, baby. You're valued not just by how much you mean to people—and you mean the world to a lot of us—but by how much you mean to yourself.

You should remember that, all right?" Auntie says, taking my hand in hers.

"All right," I say, just wanting this whole talk to stop.

"Don't make that face at me, girl. I'm trying to have a moment with you." Auntie laughs.

But the moment's over, and soon we're laughing and talking like regular for the rest of the night together.

When we're getting ready for bed, Auntie puts cocoa butter on my elbows and looks at me in the mirror.

"You look like her, you know that?" Auntie says.

"My mom?" I ask. And then I quickly correct myself: "Janet?" I've never seen that. Janet is beautiful when she wants to be. She's sleek and tall, and she moves like she's on a runway even when she's just going to the bodega. She's perfect in those moments, and I'm never perfect, not like that.

"Yes. Girl, look." Auntie takes my head in her hands and points my face toward the mirror. "Look at this nose. And these cheeks. That's Janet to a T!"

I keep looking in the mirror trying to see it, but I can't. Or maybe I don't want to, it's hard to say.

"You thinking about her?" Auntie asks, putting cocoa butter on her elbows now.

"A little," I lie.

"She'll be home soon, don't worry."

And just like that I've ruined everything.

The next morning, I get up early to leave bottles again for Jen. It's a smaller bag than what we usually have at my house, but I figure it's still a nice thing to do for Jen and her grandmother. Well, it's not just that. It's also that I haven't seen Jen since I told her my mother was a drunk and ran off like a crazy person. I'd like to explain a little, or at least tell her the whole truth. It's strange how you can feel so close to someone you barely know.

I take the blue plastic bags of bottles out the front door and sit on the front steps to wait for them. But after ten minutes, then fifteen, they haven't come. I want to wait longer, but then it's getting late and I have to get to school. Ducks comes out of his house, but instead of coming up to mine, he just stops and stares at me. I've been avoiding him at the end of the day, and it's unfair, I know. He puts in both earbuds and walks down to 7th Avenue without me.

I run in to grab my books and race after him, but by the time I get back, he's already gone. I'll have to try to talk to him later.

CHAPTER 14

Allegra starts passing me notes, leaving them hanging from my locker all morning. Usually they're about something we're doing, something she saw, or if we're walking home together, but today they're all about Ryan. I thought that she'd be mad about me walking home with him every day this week, like Ducks is, but it's not that. It's not that at all. It's something closer to excited. It feels jealous, but it's not that clear. The last note she leaves tells me she misses me and wants to know if she can walk with us, or if we can walk to her house and get dinner or something. She's asking both of us, Ryan and me, like that's a thing now. After I read it, I'm more confused than anything.

It's so weird to see Allegra interested in something that isn't herself or on her phone. When I see her at lunch, she's staring at me, like she's wondering if I read the note and how I will react. I smile, because I guess that's what she needs, and she returns a huge smile that almost makes me think she's making fun of me. She comes over to the table and she's being super nice to me, paying more attention to everything I say and looking at me the whole time. When she does talk, it's mostly about Ryan.

"So you, like, think Ryan would go for that? Like, coming to my house? It wouldn't be a big deal, would it?" She's almost nervous as she says this part. I still don't get what any of this is about. I can't believe I'm saying it, but I wish Allegra would stop looking at me.

"Well, if he wants to come with us, he can. I'm not in charge of him. You can ask," I answer. She seems a little bit disappointed at first, then confused.

"But will it be okay, if you just walk with me?" Allegra says, looking at the floor, like she's hiding something.

"I don't have to report in," I say. "Why don't I come over tonight? I'll just have to check in with my aunt. She's the only one that matters."

Allegra looks at me again, but now with big happy eyes. "That would be the Best Evah."

"Cool," I say, trying not to show her how weirded out I am by her. She's just being so silly.

After lunch, Ducks is telling a funny story to Ellen. He's waving his hands around and making Ellen smirk. I smile, knowing how funny he is, and miss him. I wish I were over with them right now. When he sees me looking at him, he stops the story and walks away. Ellen looks confused, he probably wasn't even done with the story yet. She looks over at me and shakes her head. We both shrug at each

106

other and she chases him into their next class. I need to talk to him. It gets me a little angry that I have to. Why can't he just relax for a minute?

After class, Ryan walks up to my locker to see how my day is going, which is really sweet, but today it just seems like too much. I feel like everyone around me needs something, and all I really need is to get home while home is still safe.

"You okay?" Ryan asks, leaning over my open locker door.

"Yeah," I answer with a big huff.

"Okay? I was just saying hi." Ryan smiles, hoping that will get me to smile back. It's a cute smile, I just don't like it right now.

"I can't walk home today," I say, closing my locker. I can't tell if it's the sound of the door or the way that I'm saying it, but either way he blinks like he's been hit in the head. I feel bad, because I don't want to hurt him, but I just need a little less today. "It's not a big deal. I just have to hang out with Allegra tonight."

That seems to soften it a little, but then he asks, "Well, can I come by for a bit?"

"No. It's just a girls' night. I don't think Allegra would like it," I answer. I know that's not the truth, and I know I just lied to Ryan, but right now, it's just the easiest way to handle this. Ryan seems really hurt, but I smile at him, trying to tell him it's not a big deal. I just have to keep them apart for a bit, because it's such a silly thing to lie about and that will only make it a bigger deal for everybody involved.

At the end of the day, Ryan goes out the side door, so I head out the front with Allegra. I'm pulling her so hard she almost squeaks. And because I must be having a really lucky week, a cab pulls right by, and with one hand I wave it over and with the other I push her into the back seat. We're gone so quick Ryan doesn't even see us leave.

At Allegra's house, Kylie is already home, so right off we're headed for trouble. She's listening to music and reading. She takes a big bite of a pear just as we walk in, like she's about to take a bite out of Allegra. She says something awful to Allegra but then looks at me.

"Great outfit. Very, very."

I don't want to be so excited by Allegra's sister, but I can't help myself. Kylie's cool, high-school cool, so in ways that I don't even know about yet. I sound like Ducks and his adjectives, but it's true. I'd act more excited but she's so mean to Allegra, I think it would make Allegra furious with me. So I just smile and wait until they blow up at each other. Any minute, they'll be screaming and cursing. Sometimes it gets to pulling hair, a few times even punches, but hopefully not now. I follow Allegra out to the kitchen.

"Did you eat all the yogurt?" Allegra positively screams from the refrigerator, banging on the door.

"Go get your own," Kylie screams from the living room.

"That *was* my own! I wrote my name on it. Mom!" Allegra screams and slams the fridge. Allegra's mom doesn't answer. Allegra marches up the stairs to her room and I follow. It isn't until we hit the landing that we hear her mom yell, "What's wrong? What happened?"

"She ate all my yogurt!" Allegra yells back from her doorway.

"Allegra, stop," her mother shouts. "We can get you more yogurt. You're being ridiculous."

Allegra's mom keeps yelling at her and at Kylie downstairs, but Allegra ignores her. She waves me into her room, slamming the door behind me.

"So, Ryan couldn't come?" Allegra says when the yelling outside stops.

"Yeah. He had to go home. It's cool, just us, right?" I ask.

"Totally. I was, like, more thinking of you anyway." Allegra smirks a little. "You guys are, like, going out now. You must want to be around him all the time."

"We're walking home from school, Leg. It's not like we're getting married."

"Okay, but it's still serious. You're, like, a full teenager now," Allegra says, almost rolling her eyes at me.

"What's going on with Brian?" I ask. I know there isn't much, but I'm sort of mad at her for acting like this.

"He's fine. I think he's, like, way too immature for me. He picks his nose." Allegra smiles a little to hard to mean it. "But Ryan is so different, you can, like, see he, like, cares about you. Like, a hundred percent."

"He's nice."

"You're, like, super lucky and everyone is, like, so jealous."

I want to ask if everyone includes her. But I don't want to actually fight with her. I don't feel like I'm some different or older person now. Why does she even care? And why is she talking about me with people?

"Have you kissed yet?" Allegra asks.

"No," I yell. Allegra laughs at how loud I'm being, but I don't care.

"You should. I bet he's, like, a great kisser," Allegra says, turning on her laptop. How would Allegra know about him anyway? Allegra starts watching makeup tutorials, so for at least a little while we can pretend to be thinking about other things, but the whole time I just want to know what we're really doing here. Are we in a fight? Because it feels like we are.

When we get called down for dinner, I'm trying to forget about our weirdness or at least ignore it. Allegra's mom doesn't cook, so we order Indian and just take it back up to her room to watch more videos. Allegra and Kylie have an argument over a piece of naan that ends up with a slap. Besides that, it all goes by pretty smoothly.

But the minute we get back to Allegra's room, she starts in about Ryan again. Or rather, she just wants to know how I feel about him. How does he make me feel when we're together? What do I think about going out with a boy like him? She's asking me like she thinks there's something I know that she can't find out for herself. But I don't and I can't understand why she's treating me like this. Most of it I answer, always trying to change the subject, until she says, "It's like you're a whole different person now."

"What does that mean?" I ask, already angry.

"I'm not, like, saying it to be mean." Allegra stops. "I'm just saying that it's like you're on a different, like, level now. Like you're higher above the rest of us because you have a boyfriend."

"I don't have a boyfriend, Leg," I answer, harder than I'd like but wanting to make it really clear to her.

"Okay, but why can't you just be, like, happy about it?" Allegra says. "I would be."

I don't answer that because I was going to say something so mean to her. I just fake a text from my aunt and take the subway home. When I get there, Auntie is sitting in the kitchen and looking at the photo album she brought from her apartment.

"How was your friend's? Did they feed you?" she says, smiling but still looking at the book.

"Yes, I'm fine," I answer.

"There's corn bread on the counter if you want. I got lonesome for something real like that, looking at these." She draws me over and brushes a few braids from my face. She's looking at a picture of my mother. At least I think it's my mother. It's black and white, and the girl in it is shading her eyes from the sun.

"Is that Janet?" I say, pointing at the picture.

"Yes," Auntie Amara says, kissing my cheek.

"Where are you?" I ask.

"I took the picture. Your mama was the pretty one."

I don't know why, but that makes me sadder than anything that's happened today. It's not what was said, but what wasn't. Pretty seems like a rotten thing to be.

CHAPTER 15

Because I feel bad about lying to him, I walk home with Ryan again. It's a nice thing too. I like him, but it's weird that you can talk to a person and hold their hand and walk home with them for days, and still they can know you so little. He doesn't really ask about me. He tells me a lot, and I like listening.

His hand is still clammy, but I almost find that cute now. And he repeats his stories. I mean, I feel like I've heard about him getting lost in the park at least three times. When he asks about my day, he asks questions that I think a boyfriend or whatever should ask, but they're just silly things. He never gets into anything else, and even if he did I don't know what I would tell him.

There's still nothing from Janet. I've gotten so used to being without her, I sometimes forget she's coming back. Ryan doesn't know any of this. He just smiles his cutest goofy smile when I leave him at the gate. I should really ask him in, but I put it off. I can let Auntie meet him another day. He's talking a lot about going to the movies tomorrow night. He's super excited about it, but I don't know what he's expecting us to do. I mean besides the movie. We're thirteen and neither of us has money to go into Manhattan or go out to dinner or anything. I'm trying not to laugh at how serious he's taking all this when a lady with her dog walks past us and gives us a look.

She stares at us for a minute before she starts pretending she wasn't. She starts to look at where her little dog might go, but she's really just pretending not to be staring at us, which has her one step away from fully rolling her eyes or saying *eww*. Ryan doesn't notice any of this. He wouldn't even if he saw it, but I do because I know exactly what she's doing. None of her covering hides it from me.

Every day you go out in the world and you're just like everybody else, at least you think you are. Maybe you have things worse than others, maybe your mother is a crazy screaming drunk who cares more about organizing her issues of *Vogue* than about feeding herself or you. Maybe you have to get up early to sneak out all her bottles without anyone noticing and only tell the truth to an embarrassed girl whose grandmother is digging through your trash. The specifics of your day might be different or unusual, but deep down you're just like everybody else. You're normal, if there's even such a thing as normal at all. But then some old lady walking her dog stops cold and takes a minute to let you know that no, you're not normal, you're black.

And you're holding a white boy's hand near Prospect Park, and that's not normal either.

I hate this old lady. I hate her stupid face the minute I look at her, and I do look back at her, hard. I look back in her stupid face, to let her know that I know exactly what she thinks she's doing. She thinks she's getting away with it, but she's not and I want her to know it. I want her to feel as bad as she's trying to make me feel. I want her to know how stupid and small and piggish she is. I even want her stupid dog to know. I almost want to kick it. But then I think it probably doesn't know it's owned by an idiot.

It's only a second, and nothing is actually said. Unless someone's looking for something, they probably wouldn't notice, but I do. I know it, and I know it's real. It's the one thing I actually learned from my mother. Janet gets furious about stuff like this when it happens. And it happens more than you would think. She stands up for herself. She never allows anyone to make her feel like this. It's why no one talks to her in the little Korean grocery down the street from our house.

I want to scream and shout like Janet. I even wish she was here to do it for me, but she isn't. I'm angry and sad, and I want to cry as much as I want to fight, but the worst part is how embarrassed I feel. I feel like I've done something wrong, or that I'm somewhere I'm not supposed to be. But none of that's true. We're walking to my house, past the park that I've been in a thousand times. There's nothing wrong. I'm just black, and this lady wants me to know it and know that she doesn't approve.

I'm quiet for the rest of the walk home. Ryan notices but doesn't ask me about it. I feel bad because I'm sure that he's thinking it's about him and that I don't want to go out with him on Friday, but I don't feel bad enough to tell him what really happened. I squeeze his clammy hand and wave to him twice before I go inside, but I really can't do much more. I'm still a little too angry.

The house is empty, and it makes me feel almost worse. I don't want to be alone with this any longer than I have to be. In the kitchen, there's a big pot on the stove and a note taped to it.

Sophie,

I had to run up to my apartment to grab a few things. I should be back by the time you get home, but in case I'm not there's stew here for you. Heat it up and eat it up.

Love you,

Auntie Amara

It doesn't seem like much, but at the moment, it's the nicest thing anyone could have done for me. I fold the note and put it in my pocket to keep forever. I turn on the stove and get out bowls and spoons before I even feel the tears in my eyes. It's a sad moment, but a happy moment at the same time. I just wish I wasn't alone for it.

Auntie Amara comes through the door about an hour later, calling, "Sophie, come help me with these bags." Standing in the hallway, she gives me an exhausted smile and scoots a large bag of books into the hallway with her foot.

"Why didn't you take the schlepper with you?" I ask her, happy to help.

"I didn't know I would take this much. Once I started pulling, I just couldn't stop. There's another bag outside," Auntie Amara says as she carries a heavy bag over to the foot of the steps. I squeeze past her and head out the front door to grab the other books. It's cold, so I jump down the stairs to get the books in before I need a jacket.

Back inside, Auntie's already stirring the stew, with music blasting, and the feelings I had while alone start to melt away. I drop the bag of books and run out to the kitchen. I want to be with her, and I want to talk. I talk to Auntie Amara not like I'd talk to an adult, where I leave out the details of what I'm really thinking or clean up the language so they don't think I'm stupid or dirty. But I don't talk to her like a friend either. It's something in the middle. I tell her more than I thought I would, but there's still a bunch I didn't say. I don't mention the lady by the park. I don't want to get mad again.

"Why did you change your name?" I ask her, out of nowhere.

"What, baby?" Auntie smiles. I think she heard me, but she might be stalling to answer me, which makes me worry that I've asked the wrong question and ruined everything. I have to repeat it now or I'll make it worse.

"Why did you change your name?" I ask again, looking down, hoping that if I have screwed up she will at least forgive me because I look sorry.

"It's a powerful thing to take a name, Miss Sophie." She smiles. "I hope you get to do it one day."

Auntie wipes down the counter as she talks to me and tells me all about it. "I never felt like Sheryl. I mean, do I look like a Sheryl to you? I do not. It was a name my mother gave me to be respectable, but I didn't know that I wanted to be respectable. It got to the point that even the sound of *Sheryl* would turn my stomach. Sheryl. Oh, you shouldn't ever hate the sound of your own name. And I did. I hated it. Or maybe I just hated what it meant.

"Your grandmother Adelaide was a tough old lady. She terrorized your mother. I got off easier, but that's only by a matter of degrees."

"Is Adelaide alive?" I ask. Janet always says mean things about her mother, but I've never actually heard her name.

"No, your grandmother died about four years ago," Auntie says. "I'm not mad at her anymore. She had a tough time of it. Took a lot on her shoulders, raising us girls all alone. My father died when I was eight and your mama was about six. And she did the best she could by us. We were fed and had clean clothes. Both of her girls went to college. But so much of how we spoke to each other was set out to hurt the other person. It wasn't a fun place to be." As she says this, she's laughing, but the sound of her laugh changes a bit, like she's trying to distract me from actually listening.

"I went to Spelman College. Your mother went right to New York and never went back. I couldn't blame her for that. Adelaide was at her all the time. Watching her, picking at her, just mean and jealous. I was a thick girl and dark as a berry, so she didn't pay me half the mind she did to Janet. I don't know which was worse.

"It wasn't until I was away at school that I even knew I was smart. I got the first taste of being on my own, got the first taste being seen as a person with my own thoughts and wants and beauty, maybe. I'd wanted that feeling forever.

"I wanted to be my own person, I wanted my life to be my own, and part of that was naming myself for myself. It might sound a little silly, but Sheryl? That's the name of some sickly little thing sitting in an office in Minnesota. I'm a dark, thick intelligent woman and I need a name that lets everyone know that I love every inch, every dimple on my fat black brilliant butt. So I picked Amara. It means *grace* in Igbo.

"I was reclaiming myself. Who I knew I was inside, or who I would turn myself into. My name came from Africa, where I was from, from a language that fit into the grooves of my mouth and that was and is very important to me. Your mama hates it," Auntie says, laughing and clapping her hands loudly. "She thinks I'm putting something on. That I had to make myself special in some extra way because Sheryl just wasn't cutting it. And you know what, she's probably right to a degree, but so what if she is? I deserve to be a little special, don't you think?"

I agree, nodding and laughing along.

"She was mostly mad because she thought I didn't like white people."

"Don't you?" I ask. It's the first time I'm nervous during the whole conversation.

"I do. It's like how I felt about my mother. Sure, she was mean and grouchy, and I could only take about a five-minute phone call at a time, or I'd be breaking plates in my apartment, which is pretty stupid, because they're my plates, but behind all that, I loved her. I wanted her to be well and happy, as happy as she could be. I want the same for white people. I just know how much I can take. Janet never thought I liked your father."

"He's a jerk," I say out loud, and I immediately cover my mouth because I have never really said anything so honest to anyone. Auntie hoots at me twice and hits me with a dishcloth as she continues to laugh.

"He is, and it's not because he's white. It just doesn't help." Auntie laughs here the loudest. We both do.

"In some ways, you never get to choose the people you love. You don't choose who you're born to, or where or when. You have to deal with that and get over it. But you can always choose who you let in, and you can always choose who you want to be. You're your own creation, baby, and don't let anyone in the world tell you different."

"I won't." I smile. I believe it. I believe it so much and want to even more.

Auntie Amara reaches over and holds me hard. I resist it a little at first. Auntie's body is so big against mine that I feel like I have to pull back just to still feel like myself, but after a few seconds I settle into her. I squeeze hard against her and hold on.

Before I can stop myself, I say, "Please don't leave me," into her shoulder. As the words tumble out of my mouth, so do tears. Tears that burn my face, because I've been fighting them back for years.

"Janet is a drunk. And I hate her."

CHAPTER 16

The next few hours go by in soggy faces and words and words and words that I barely believe I'm saying. But it's me telling Auntie everything. All the screaming and crying and the mess, then the apologizing that never leads to anything. All the nights I'm alone in my room waiting for her just to pass out. How it all happens over and over again and it never feels like it's ever going to get better. It all pours out, faster than I can handle. I say things that are true but sound made-up because I've never spoken the words out loud before. It is almost like someone else is talking about the broken bottles and screaming and the fights. It's the voice of someone older and much more aware of everything, someone tired and frustrated and lonely. But as every word gets unstuck from the back of my throat, I know the voice is mine.

Auntie holds my hand and listens, brushing tears away from my cheek with her milky palm and asking me questions when she can.

"How long has it been like this?"

"How did you get her up the stairs?"

"Did she hit you hard?"

None of Auntie's questions are meant to stop me, like so many adults would want to do in this situation. They would want to tell me something, or teach me something, or make me understand something about what's been going on with Janet, but Auntie does none of that. It's the first time, ever, in my life that I feel like a person on my own. And it makes me want to say even more.

When it's done, or at least when I can't say any more over the sobs gurgling up in my throat, she holds me close again and rocks me in the softness of her body. I cry the way a baby cries because it doesn't know any words, because for me there aren't any words left. When I lift my face, there's a huge wet mark on Auntie's shirt where I used to be. She sees it, but says nothing and holds my face in her hands. There are more important things.

"I am so sorry, baby," Auntie cries to me.

"You don't have anything to be sorry about." I sniffle.

"You shouldn't have had to do this alone. I should have been there for you, and I wasn't." Auntie starts to cry now too.

We sit there for hours with each other. I want to take away her tears, because it's not her fault, and I love her. I want to tell her that there was nothing she could have done, because with Janet, there wasn't room for anyone else. The house has been crowded with her drinking for so long, it feels like there's barely enough room for me. My whole life has been wondering how much has she had, how will it all hit her, or how long will I have until the next explosion. There have been whole years of what now and what next.

The worst part is that I never saw it ending before now. I'd gotten so used to the rhythm of it that I could count the days like a formula, and numbers are always honest. Sure, sometimes she'd surprise me, but even then within seconds I'd know what I was up against and I knew I could handle it. It sounds bizarre to say, but I was proud of myself for that. But then there's the embarrassment and the shame of it, all the time. The lying that she does, drinking booze out of coffee cups in the daytime to pretend she isn't getting drunk, and acting overly nice to everyone she talks to on the phone. Even the lie of the front living room. Look how fancy and clean and white this room is, could somebody that passes out in the same clothes for three days and throws up every other morning have a nice room like this? Could they? It's off-limits to both of us, because we both are keeping up the lie.

But why?

Because . . . and this is the part that makes me cry the loudest, it's because I love her. I love Janet more than anyone else in the world. It's hard to remember that sometimes, but the truth is that I did it because I love her. I don't like her a lot, but I love her more than anything.

I love the way her nose twitches when she's about to say something funny, and Janet says so much that is funny. On good nights when she's happy drunk and just yelling at the TV, she's usually funnier than anything on it. And she's smart, so smart, she can talk to you about anything in the world, and explain these huge ideas to you in the simplest terms, so it seems so basic and straightforward. She never makes you feel like you couldn't understand it without her. She's just catching you up.

And beautiful. My mother, Janet, is beautiful. *Elegant* is the word, really. She's long and tall like a model, but beautiful in a warmer way. She's not an icy thing walking down the runway just to show off the clothes, she's not just a fleshy hanger. She's a person you want to follow, you want to watch her move, half because you can't believe someone does everything so well, but half because you're hoping that some of it will rub off on you. At least I do. Try as hard as I can, I can't hate her, because even in her worst moments, there's a hint of this funny, smart, and beautiful woman somewhere deep inside. She's drowning in vodka, and part of me always wants to save her.

It gets so late after a while that both of us head up to bed. I brush my teeth and look out into the hall to see Auntie in my mother's room. "You want to sleep in here with me? You're not too big, are you?" Auntie smiles at me, patting my mother's bed.

It seems like such a strange thing to do. I don't ever remember sleeping with my mother, even as a little kid. I mean, when I was really small, my father would never have allowed it, and after he left, it wasn't anything I ever even thought of. Janet and I are separate people with separate beds, but now, seeing Auntie pat her bed and smile, I think it might be fun. I mean, I never got to do it as a kid, so I probably have at least one of these moments owed to me. So I walk into Janet's room and sit on the bed.

"Go on, get under the covers."

Auntie turns off the light and leans back onto the bed. I can feel it shift as she turns over to me.

"You're a very brave little girl, you know that?" Auntie says.

"I'm not," I say to her, looking at the ceiling in the darkness.

"You are. I'm here for you, and I promise I always will be. Okay?"

I say okay as I turn on my side and move closer to her. She puts her arm around me and tells me she loves me. Her arm is warm in parts and cold in others, but it all feels good, and faster than I think I ever have before, I fall right to sleep.

The next morning, I'm tired for sure, but waking up with Auntie's arm still around me seems worth it. I try to sneak out of the room without waking her, but by the time I get to the door, she's up. "Do you want me to make you eggs or something?"

"No, I'm all right," I answer. I really want to let her sleep, I already feel like I've kept her up enough. I expect things to be different or heavier this morning, but it actually feels like the opposite. I smile at Auntie to thank her and to show her that I'm all right. I need to get ready for school.

It's early and I don't have to leave right away, so I sit in the quiet kitchen and have a glass of orange juice all alone at the island. I don't turn on the TV or look at my phone. I just like the quiet of the house and knowing that it's a good quiet rather than the quiet of waiting until something horrible happens.

Outside, it's getting colder than I expected, so I'm glad I wore a sweater but wish I would have worn a hat with it or something. I walk past Ducks's house just as he's coming out the front door with wet hair that will freeze on his way to school. He never dresses warm enough, and I really don't know why.

He stops in the doorway when he sees me, so I stop too.

"Hey," I call over the wrought-iron fence.

"Hey," he answers, closing the door behind him.

"Are you walking?" I ask.

"Yeah," he answers again, lifting the side of his lips to say this so it drags out much longer than the word would otherwise.

"Do you mind if I walk with you?" I ask as he almost gets to the gate.

"Sure," he says, doing the lip thing again and squeezing past me through the gate. He starts off without me, but I follow him, walking as fast as he's walking, if only a little behind. We don't say a word to each other until we're a few blocks down 7th Avenue.

"Did you do the math?" I ask. It's the first thing I can really think to say. There is this thing with Ducks that makes me nervous and it always has. He knows me. He knows me better than almost anyone else in the world, but he doesn't always trust how well he knows me. And the worst part about that is that out of everyone, he's the only one who should. I'd never give him up for Ryan. I'd never give him up.

I start things off gentle and off subject, but he knows that I'm hedging toward what we actually both want to talk about. Math homework is a great place to start.

"I just don't get math and I don't know why I even have to." He shrugs.

"Well, you don't want to fail," I spit back at him.

"No, but I just think, at a certain point, we have to be able to say that there are certain things we're just not good at and be fine about it."

"And this is that point, eighth grade?" I laugh.

"Yeah, why not? I mean seriously, when in my whole life am I ever, ever going to use algebra? So let's just all cut it out already," Ducks says, laughing. He's so funny when he wants to be. I know part of it is that he's being serious, but it's how he says these crazy things that just makes me laugh. It always has.

"Well, what else?" I laugh.

"Gym. I mean, who cares? I don't want to know what a football is, and I don't want to learn how to throw it."

"Okay. No gym. What else?" I ask.

"Well, like, geography seems pretty dumb, and chemistry. Those sort of suck too."

"Well, what does that even leave you? English."

"Social studies with Mr. Gennetti," says Ducks.

"Well, of course you're going to pick that." I laugh so loud, rolling my eyes. I wait for the laugh after, but it doesn't come. He's not pouting, but he's just looking down. He seems sad about it but almost in a different way than I've ever really seen him. It's a sadness that's colder, it stops the air around him. It's like he's shrinking in front of me, going to a small place that I can't see.

To shake him out of it, I swing my arm through his, and push him forward, step after step, catching up with him and then pushing him forward again, talking about what I would get rid of, and telling him what I would keep. Saying that Mr. Gennetti is cute, if you like that sort of guy, but he's just not my type.

"Ryan's your type." Ducks smiles at me shyly.

"I . . . maybe." I smile back. "I'm sorry about before."

"Yeah." Ducks smiles again. "I really love your new hair."

And I know that's all we'll say about it. I would like to say that I'm sorry for hurting his feelings, because I am actually sorry about that, but it's so hard to keep up with all the feelings and fears and worries Ducks has. It's not so hard that I'd give up, just on some rounds I need to sit one out. I hope he trusts that I'll always come back.

CHAPTER 17

At the last bell, I race down the stairs to meet Ryan. When he comes out the side door, he takes my hand right away, which is a little more in-your-face than it has been on the other days we walked home together, but I don't mind. I guess he's thinking tonight is a big deal.

Everything is pretty much the same until we get to my street, and we see Ellen and Ducks walking from the far corner. I'm not embarrassed to be holding Ryan's hand or anything, even though both their faces totally change when they see it. Ellen looks at us first, then looks away, but Ducks just stares, almost curious about it. Ryan gets nervous, I can feel his palm get wetter the closer we get to them.

I wave to them, hoping that will help us all. Ellen waves back as she pulls Ducks, still staring, through the gate to his house and up the stairs to his front door. I laugh at how rough she is with him. It all seems so silly.

Ryan stops by my front gate. "So do you want me to walk over here first or is it easier just to meet at the movie theater?" He smiles, looking at his shoes and peeking up at me.

"I can meet you there. It's closer to your house anyway."

"Sure, but seriously, I, like, don't care about that," Ryan says, looking up at me a little more. "I just want to do whatever you want to do."

"Okay. So I will just meet you there." I smile and head through the gate.

"I'll be there at seven, is that good?" Ryan says.

"Yeah. Perf." I wave goodbye as I get to the top of the stairs.

Inside the house, I hear Auntie in the kitchen. I drop my things in the hallway and head in to talk to her.

"Hey, baby. How was school?" Auntie says, without looking up at me from her laptop. She's busy, working I guess, but I don't mind. And just when I actually wonder whether I mind or not, she looks up, takes off her glasses, and smiles at me. There's nothing else to it. She seems to always know what I need.

"I'm making chicken tonight, it should be done in about an hour, is that all right?" she asks, closing the computer.

"You don't have to do that. I know you have work," I say, going over to the refrigerator to get a glass of water.

"I do have work, and I will have it. So don't worry about that. Now tell me how, was your day?" Auntie smiles and waits for me to tell her every detail about nothing that is worth repeating, but I at least try. Halfway through algebra, Auntie checks the chicken, and I have to tell her that I'm going out tonight.

"What's this, now?" Auntie says, standing up from the open oven door.

"I'm going to the movies with Ryan."

"Who's Ryan?" Auntie smiles, but I think there's more to it.

"He's the boy who's been walking me home. It's not a big deal," I say, drinking my water and looking right at her, knowing that if I look down at any moment she will think there's a lot more to it than I'm telling her, and that's just not the case at all.

"That boy, huh?" Auntie says, closing the oven. "I got eyes, little sister, and I got ears, too, so you better start talking." There's a small laugh in her voice, so I don't think she's totally angry, but it's only a small laugh. I don't want to lose it completely.

"It's not like a date," I say quietly and calmly.

"Who said 'date'? You did." Auntie smiles. "What time is he coming to pick you up?"

"He's not, I'm meeting him at the movie theater at the end of the park."

"Oh, no, you're not. No way. If you're going out with this boy, I want to talk to him first," Auntie says, moving away from the oven. "I should have met him already, walking you home every day. So now I have to step in."

"But I said I would just meet him there, it's closer to his house," I say, getting a little angry. Why is she not being cool about this?

"Well, un-tell him. Or I can," she says, picking up her phone. I know she doesn't even have his number, but still it makes me nervous enough to grab mine quickly and text Ryan.

> Can you come and pick me up? My aunt wants you to.

Ok. Is she mad or something?

> No, she just wants to meet you. She's pretty chill. It won't be a big deal, I totally swear.

Ok. I'll be to you by 6:30.

> Ok. Thanks.

Np

The whole time I'm texting Ryan, Auntie keeps asking me all sorts of questions about him and answering them before I get a chance. Does his mother know where you're going? Is he a nice boy? Well, a nice boy would have introduced himself already, and that's the real truth. But does he do all right in school? Is he smart? Not too smart to try to take you out and meet you at the theater without even a hello to me.

I look up and try to stop her, but there's no stopping her. I'm starting to get angry with Auntie. Or maybe disappointed. Everyone is making a big deal out of this, when it is exactly the opposite of a big deal. I try to answer everything she has to say with one- or two-word answers, and I run up the stairs the first chance I get.

I take a shower and start to get ready. I pick a vintage corduroy dress that hangs low over a pair of patterned leggings. I wear bracelets, which I feel good about. A pair of little black ballet shoes instead of dark high-tops.

When I come back down the stairs, Auntie's waiting for me. "Oh, girl, you look good, turn around." She takes my hand to twirl me around and see the whole look.

"I like your hair up," she says.

"Thanks," I say, getting out of the twirl and finding my way to a stool to sit down.

"What time is Ryan coming to pick you up?" Auntie says, sitting down on her own stool and moving an already made-up plate toward me.

"Six thirty," I say, looking for a napkin. Auntie takes a roll of paper towels and rips me off a big piece, which she tucks into my dress. I feel stupid, like a baby, but I don't get mad about it, I just want to get out of here in one piece. And she's nice to worry about my look. She asks me lots about Ryan while we eat, and I answer the best I can, but there's a lot I don't know.

"You don't know what his parents do?" Auntie says loudly as I'm trying to finish my peas.

"We don't talk about that stuff," I answer.

"Well, what do you talk about?"

"I don't know. School? Basketball?"

"What do you know about basketball?" Auntie laughs but then gets very serious. "Would your mother let you go out with this boy?"

When she asks this one, I look at her, right in her face, for a bit. I don't know. I probably wouldn't have told her. She probably wouldn't have asked. This wouldn't have been a big deal to her, and for that and only for that, in this moment, I almost miss her.

"I don't know," I answer.

"I have a responsibility to watch you. To your mother and to you. I know you don't think of it that way, but I do. I owe you a lot more care than you give yourself, little sister. So I am going to talk to this Ryan, and I'm going to set him straight when it comes to you, you got me?"

"You don't have to do that," I say loudly.

"I do," Auntie Amara repeats until I stop arguing. "I'm not going to embarrass you or him, you're at the age when this stuff starts happening. So I get that, but you have to understand, and so does this white boy, that there are boundaries."

"Why do you have to call him a white boy?" I ask, trying not to get angry.

"Isn't that what he is?" Auntie looks at me. She clears the plates once we finish and washes them by herself because she doesn't want me to ruin my outfit.

"Do you like him?" she asks from the sink.

"Yes," I say.

"How much?" she asks.

"I don't know, enough?" I say, not really knowing what else to say.

"Well, all right then. If you're not going to give me a solid answer, I will just have to wait until Ryan, the white boy, shows up here." I don't want to, but I have to laugh at that.

At 6:28 p.m., the doorbell rings. I know because we're both watching the clock waiting for Ryan. I start to get up to answer it, but even before I can get off the stool, Auntie puts her hand up and walks past me to answer it herself. I stay on the stool, because I don't know what else to do. I hear them at the door. Ryan is polite and asks for me. Auntie tells him he can call her Dr. Watley and brings him into the kitchen.

I see that he's definitely thinking this is a big deal tonight. He's got gel or something slick in his hair and a gerbera daisy for me. He looks so stiff and scared that I don't really know how to help him in this moment.

"Does your mother know you're taking my niece out on a date, young man?" Auntie asks him.

"Yes, Dr. Watley. She does. She told me she was fine with it as long as I was home by ten," Ryan says, looking at her, but sneaking a peek at me. He tries to smile. But he's still a little freaked out.

"Well, it's good she trusts you. I hope you won't let either of us down," Auntie says. "You look nervous, Ryan. Am I making you nervous?"

"A little," Ryan says, handing the gerbera daisy to me and smiling.

"Good." Auntie smiles and says to Ryan, "Go wait by the door and I will send her out."

Ryan looks at me in a panic, but I smile, trying to ease him out of the room. He goes slowly, looking back at me and my aunt until he's by the kitchen door. Auntie waits until he's out of earshot and tosses her hand at me as if asking her pocketbook.

"Here's forty dollars for the movie and a cab ride home. I don't want you walking home at ten. And you text what movie you're seeing and when it gets out. You hear me?" Auntie says, digging in her pocketbook.

"Yes," I say, getting off the stool for the first time.

"Have a fun time and behave yourself." She smiles and yells out to the hallway, "That goes doubly for you, Ryan."

I slowly walk down the hall to the front door, speeding up only when I get to Ryan, grabbing his arm and heading out the door, before Auntie can say anything else. Outside alone, and a little cold, we both start to laugh, which is nice. Because at least if this is a "thing," it can be a fun "thing." Can't it?

CHAPTER 18

Ryan talks a lot on the way to the movies. His breath freezes as it puffs out in front of his face, like he's a train speeding off to somewhere else. I nod along, not that I'm not interested, but because I don't totally know what to say or talk about now that I know this is a "thing." If it was just the movies, or even a walk, I could talk about something when and if Ryan asked me. But now there's a flower and he met my auntie and cab money is in my pocket. It's a thing and I don't know what you're supposed to say on a thing.

We make it to the theater pretty quickly and look through what movies they're showing. Ryan picks a superhero something because I don't say much and I don't really care. The more I'm with him the less it seems so serious. We're laughing and talking just like after school. I hope it stays like that, I guess that will depend on us. Ryan pays for my ticket, which I keep telling him he doesn't need to do, but he keeps telling me that he wants to. It's a nice thing to do, it is, but it's also a date thing to do. I smile and head into the theater with him. His hand is clammy as he holds on to mine, even though I'm the one that's nervous.

Ryan orders popcorn and asks if I want anything, but I don't. Seriously I don't. But I also don't know if I'm supposed to eat candy or popcorn on a thing. I would have gotten gummies and a Coke and even though I said I didn't want any popcorn, I will steal his halfway through this stupid blow-'em-up movie I don't even want to see. I just order a small Sprite. Ryan lets me at least pay for that.

Ryan gets us seats while I run into the bathroom, just to look at myself and see if I'm the same, which luckily, I am. I adjust my dress and wash my hands, which are a little gunky from Ryan's clammy palm on the way over. Looking in the mirror, I remember to text Auntie about the movie and what time it gets out. But there are already like ten other texts from Ellen, Allegra, and Ducks, through Ellen, on my phone asking how it's going. I don't answer any of them, and go back in to find Ryan. Just as the previews start, I find him sitting alone in a row toward the back with his popcorn sitting on the chair next to him. I guess that's for me.

Ryan likes to laugh. It's something I should have noticed but haven't up until now. The thing is, now when he laughs, he looks over at me to make sure I'm laughing too. If I am he's happy and he laughs louder, but if I'm not he stops. Is that what I'm supposed to do all night, just laugh along with him? It seems like a lot. I smile and nod when I'm not laughing, just so he knows it's okay if he does. I don't want him to miss out on this movie he picked.

He doesn't hold my hand through the beginning of the movie,

I think because he's eating the popcorn, but about halfway through when the mutant guy finds something that will help him beat the other mutant, he wipes his hands on his jeans and puts his open palm on the seat rest between us. That's it. It just sits there and waits. He starts looking over at me, and I smile. I guess I'm missing the hint to take his hand. Finally he smiles and takes my hand and puts it in his. It's fine, I mean at this point I don't mind holding his hand. I'm kind of glad he did it. I curl my legs up underneath me and get cozy in my seat, almost putting my head on his shoulder as I watch the stupid movie. There aren't a lot of other people in the theater, but sitting with Ryan like this, it almost seems like we're the only ones. And that seems kind of nice. I guess this is a thing.

When the movie ends, the world is saved and I've held Ryan's hand throughout the entire battle. It didn't seem too bad, I think I would have even liked it, if I'd seen it with someone else and could pay more attention to it. That wasn't happening tonight. We get out of the theater and walk to the little circle across the street, where Ryan walks on the benches and loudly tells me his favorite parts of the movie.

"Did you like it?" he asks after a while.

"Sure," I say quietly.

"You don't have to," he says.

"Oh good. I didn't."

Ryan laughs at this and sits down next to me on the bench. We play with each other's hands and talk about nothing at all for a little while. He wants to go as a zombie doctor for Halloween, and I don't want to do anything like that. He also wants to go to a party at Brian's, which sounds worse. I tell him we can talk about it later, but he keeps going.

"Well, you could be my zombie nurse?" He smiles.

"Or your zombie boss," I say, laughing at him loudly. He laughs back but then he does the weirdest thing and puts his hand on my face and kisses me. I don't close my eyes at first, but once I know what's happening, I close them. I think that's what you're supposed to do.

Ryan's lips are small and wet and he moves his head around trying to poke his tongue into my mouth. He's a little nervous about it, and I guess I am too. It feels good to be this close with him. Some of that is because it's cold, but the rest is that I like him close to me. I like having his cheek on mine and his hand on my face, with my hand on his shoulder. It feels lovely and nice.

He moves away after the first kiss and smiles. I smile back, but I just want to go back to the kissing part. It makes the most sense right now. I put my head on his shoulder and listen to him talk about how much he likes me. His heart is beating a mile a minute, and he keeps crossing and uncrossing his legs, which might be from the cold but I don't know. We go back to kissing pretty quickly.

Kissing is tingly. It makes sense why in movies when the big kiss happens all that music picks up and the rest of the world fades around it, because it does sort of feel like that. The rest of the world is gone and you're lost in the kiss for a minute, when it's good. And a few times with Ryan it's good, very good even. Other times, I'm cold or one of our phones goes off. A few times our faces don't match up right, and we both laugh.

It's getting late, so I call a car and I offer to drop him off at his house, but he says he'd rather walk. When the car gets there, he kisses me one last time, and we hold on to each other a little longer than we ever have. I feel numb and a little dizzy, maybe from the cold and the kissing, and get in the car.

Alone in the car, I don't text anyone. I just sit and feel my face, which just seconds ago had Ryan near it. This was a thing and I'm glad it was. It was a sweet thing, nothing serious or life changing, just something sweet. The movie and the flower and everyone making a big deal still seem silly to me.

We get to my house in only about five minutes, but it seems longer because there's lots on my mind. I rush up to the door, trying not to be even a minute late. But at the door I stop because I start to wonder, if after all of this, if this *was* a big deal, a changing thing like everyone thinks. Will I look different? And if I do, will Auntie be able to see it? I stop for a second and breathe out a long trail of frost, then open the door and head in.

"Sophie, baby, is that you?" she calls.

I race up the stairs and find her sitting on the edge of Janet's bed, reading. She looks up at me and smiles. I smile back. "It was fine."

"Just fine? All right. You sleeping with me?" Auntie says.

"Okay," I say, heading to the bathroom. I look at myself and see that I'm still me. I feel a little older, maybe. Everything is mostly the same, but in my eyes, I see something I didn't know was there before. It's just a little flicker of happiness, and I'm excited for it. I take off my dress and fold it up. I brush my teeth and put cocoa butter on my face and arms, but I keep looking at myself, looking for the flicker in my eyes and trying to remember if it's ever been there before.

I go to Janet's room and lie down beside Auntie Amara, who's still reading.

"Did that white boy treat you well?" she asks, holding open the covers for me.

I get in and get close to her. "Yes. He did. His name is Ryan."

"I know. Good, he seemed all right." Auntie smiles. I lie close to her, the way I was close to Ryan, and listen as she reads part of her book to me. The name of the author is in bold type on the cover of the book—Zora Neale Hurston. I start to drift off as she reads.

"It had called to her to come and gaze on a mystery. From barren brown stems to glistening leaf-buds; from the leaf-buds to snowy virginity of bloom. It stirred her tremendously. How? Why? It was like a flute song forgotten in another existence and remembered again. What? How? Why? The singing she heard had nothing to do with her ears. The rose of the world was breathing out smell."

CHAPTER 19

Sleeping in my mother's bed with Auntie makes me feel even closer to her, if that's possible. The first night, it was after everything and we both needed each other. But the second, I'd just come home from my "thing" with Ryan, and I felt so different, I didn't want to be alone. I was afraid she might wake me up and send me on to my room in the middle of the night then, but she didn't. I like being there with her, close, hearing her read or ask me questions. I thought about going to my bed on my own, too, but it seems like she's enjoying the closeness as much as I am.

Saturday morning she lets me sleep in late. When I finally do wake up, she's gone. I start to worry for a minute, mostly out of habit. I get up slowly and look around the room. Even though I've been in here so many times, I've never really looked around. When I'm in here with Auntie, I don't look much past the bed. But now, alone, I start to look at all my mother's things. Her earrings and other jewelry are all laid out on her vanity by the window in neat little rows, which seems so fake to me now. How could she be this organized about anything in the world? Her closet is the same way. Even the few pictures up are all straight in a row, right down a small stretch of wall separating two windows. Two are of me, both from a long time ago, laughing and hanging on to Janet. It's strange to see these pictures because I know they had to have happened, but I don't remember them. We seem like other people now. It all reminds me of her and the thought that she'll be home soon. This is probably one of the last times I'll be in this room.

There are at least twenty or so texts from Allegra asking about last night. Each one basically says the same thing, but she almost sort of gets in fights with herself about if she should ask me or not, then gets mad at me for not answering. Ellen sent fewer texts, but hers are shorter and angrier until she's just sending question marks. Ryan texts that he had a great time and says he will text me the next morning, but he hasn't yet. I guess I should be nervous but I'm not. I just start texting the girls back.

I tell Ellen it was fine.

Just fine???

It was great.

Just great?????

Yes. I will tell you more later.

When?

Later. I'm going to Ducks's, come
over.

maybe?

With Allegra I have to get a little more involved. She wants to know what movie we saw, and when did we see it? Did he say anything about her? Anything about Brian? Did we kiss? Were there tongues? I type short answers, knowing that no matter what, I will have to answer all over again when I see her and for the next few days after that. I tell her I will call her later.

Auntie asks what I want to do today, and I tell her I'm going to Ducks's to hang out, if that's okay. "Now what boy is this?" She smiles at me.

"It's Ducks. From down the street."

"Oh, with the opera. Okay. Is it all right with his mother?" Auntie asks.

"She's at work, it'll just be his grandmother."

"Well, she's all right." Auntie smiles and laughs to herself. "Just loud." We both laugh at that because everyone knows how loud Ducks's grandmother is.

"Call me later. And be good," Auntie yells to me from the kitchen, but I'm already out the door. I'm excited to be with Ducks. Ducks'll be the most excited and easy about Ryan, even though he doesn't like him. Ducks doesn't like rough boys like Ryan, but to be totally honest, he doesn't really know Ryan at all. He just gets nervous around him.

I knock on Ducks's door hard and hear his grandmother yelling from inside. Then him yelling back and racing down the stairs to get to me before she does, as if he's afraid of what she'll say. Sometimes she does say weird stuff to me. Nothing exactly awful, just little things where she comments on my hair or my skin, saying things that are always nice but are always nice for being different, never just nice on their own. She doesn't intend to be mean, in fact I think she means just the opposite, but it gets a little uncomfortable.

Ducks, completely out of breath and smiling, finally opens the door. I smile back and walk past him into the house.

"Well, look who's this?!" Ducks's grandmother yells from the kitchen, wiping her hands and getting up from the table to come out to us. "Don't you look a sight! So grown-up, a fine young lady you are, pet. Are you hungry?"

"No, I'm fine, Mrs. Flynn. Thank you."

"Always with the manners, would that you could teach this one. Brazen and bold is him," she says, pointing to Ducks and fixing his hair with her wet hand. "Well, run up. Go on," she says, waving us away and heading back into the kitchen.

Upstairs in the living room, Ducks has laid out piles of his records on the floor. I know there is a method to it, I just don't know what it is. He's very into this music, and he's explained to me a thousand times why and how good it is and made me listen to more than I ever would have otherwise, but I honestly don't get it. I mean, I can understand that it's pretty or beautiful, and it must be hard for all those people to sing so high or loud, but it's just not my thing. I'm glad it seems to make him really happy.

"So I went to the movies with Ryan last night," I say, looking at the piles of records.

"What did you guys see?" he says, moving a few records back to the shelf.

"I think Thor was in it?" I laugh. He laughs too.

"Well, that does sort of narrow it down. Was it good?"

"I think so."

"What did you guys talk about after the movie?" He smiles.

"I don't know," I say, trying to skip to the real stuff. "It's weird because we don't really talk about much. I mean, he talks. He talks a lot. We, like, say words, but I don't know that it's ever really about anything."

"Well, what do we talk about?" Ducks smiles and moves a pile of records.

"We talk about stuff. We talk about people and, like, stuff. Don't you think?" I ask.

"Yeah, I guess so. I'm not trying to be rude or anything, honest. I'm just trying to understand," Ducks says, taking a big pile of records and standing them up on his lap. "I mean, he's a boy, maybe you should talk about Boy stuff with him."

"You're a boy." I laugh.

"Barely." Ducks laughs.

We both smile at that. I'm glad he's not a boy like Ryan, and I think he is too. Sometimes I think we know each other so well, like, to the bone of who the other person is, so that we're afraid of it, and we want the other person to have a little space. It's, like, almost too close. Maybe that's why he has to turn everything into a joke.

"I kissed Ryan last night," I say, staring at Ducks, who's still looking at his records.

"You DID?!" His eyes widen and he looks up at me.

"Okay, like, I don't want to make a big deal about it."

"It's such a big deal," he says even louder.

"It's not, it's a kiss," I say, still trying to quiet him down.

"But it's your first. Isn't it?" he says back.

"Yes," I answer.

"What was it like?" he asks, finally quietly.

"Wetter than I thought it would be, but nice." I smile.

Ducks starts being goofy about it, which helps, and making a fake fuss about it, but still I want to really talk about it with him, and when he's bugging out his eyes like this, it gets hard.

"Tongues?" he asks.

"A little." I laugh.

"Wow, do you love him?" he asks, getting quieter than I'm even asking him to be.

"I don't know. What does that even mean?" I say. And without saying a word, Ducks gets up and goes over to an organized stack of records to find exactly the one he wants and puts it on the stereo.

"This. This is what it is." He smiles to himself.

Music comes out of the big speakers, two big voices, a boy and a girl, singing in something like Italian, maybe German, it's hard to say. I see how much he loves it and how much it seems exactly like what he thinks a kiss is like, but to me it doesn't make any sense. This wasn't my kiss, and I doubt it is for anyone else.

"It's just how everything fits together. They're together. And it sounds right, it's a little like that hum, when they hit the right notes, each separate but they go together, you know?"

"It's not totally like that," I answer. "It's cold noses and spit. It's a lot different."

"Okay. So it's gross?" Ducks laughs.

"No. Not totally. It's sweet," I say, for the first time out loud.

I smile and don't say anything else. He knows what I mean, I think. But I think he wishes it was something a little bigger than sweet. Maybe I do too.

CHAPTER 20

When I get up on Sunday, there are a bunch of emails from my father, and none of them are good. His last message to me is just *call*.

He didn't even use punctuation, so he must be furious. I lie on my bed for a while, thinking of how I should handle it. It's going to be rough. It will start with, "I'm worried about you." Then I'll have to sit through a long list of everything that's wrong with me. At least what he can tell from another continent. He hasn't even seen me in two years. He was in New York about three and a half months ago, but he and Janet were fighting about something so I didn't get to see him. That was my fault too. When he gets through this long, long list, he'll tell me he misses me. It's all such a lie. But it's a lie I'm going to have to sit through and even play into. I sit for another minute wanting to put it off, until I finally turn on Skype and call my father.

"Bonjour, Sophie." My father answers on the first ring.

"Bonjour, Papa." I smile, but it's already too late. I can feel it.

And just like that, he starts in. "I'm worried about you."

I listen to him at first, but I can only stand it for so long until I say, "No, you're not. You're not worried about me." He stops. He's shocked and looking at me like he can't believe that I've actually said anything besides *I'm sorry*. He can't believe it's me saying it. He starts scrunching his nose and squinting to see me more closely. He's almost unsure that he's talking to the same little mouse that always just sits there and takes it, but he is. "If you were worried about me, you would ask how I am. You would ask me about what's going on in my life. You would ask if I was happy. But you don't. You're just worried about yourself and about how much attention I'm paying to you. If you were worried about me, you'd be nicer to me."

"Excuse me," he says, still in disbelief. I sit very still and look into the camera, just showing him over and over that it is me. I am standing up to him.

"You're angry with me because I haven't called you, but why would I?" I say right into the camera. "All you do is tell me how bad I am, and what I'm doing wrong, when you don't even know what I'm doing at all. I am happy. I'm happy and I don't need to be told by you. You don't even know me—"

"And whose fault is that?" he finally spits out. "You never call me. You're a bad daughter to me, Sophie," my father says, angrier and more hurt than I've ever seen him, but I don't care.

"And you're a terrible father to me," I scream and hang up.

He calls back, but I don't answer. He calls back again, but I don't answer that one either. He texts, but I don't write back. I'm not in the mood to fight anymore, but I'm even less in the mood to apologize. I probably am making it worse, but I just don't care. He's an ocean away and right now that's the perfect distance he needs to be. I need to get to church.

"Oh, there you are. I didn't even hear you come down. Well, you ready?" Auntie smiles, looking in her purse, but the smile is for me. Or at least half. "You have your MetroCard?"

I don't tell my auntie about what happened with my father. I don't want him to ruin another minute of my day. We walk down the block and stop Ducks's grandmother on her way out the door.

"Don't you two look like you're heading to a fashion show! Where are you off to?" she yells down to us.

"Church," Auntie calls up to her.

"Aren't you a good one to go to church with your auntie, Sophie, love. Do you think I could get the little prince to come along with me but once? No, sir. He's still in his bed, he is."

"Well, I'm sure we all wish we could sleep in some Sundays." Auntie smiles at Mrs. Flynn.

"Well, we wish for a million-dollar check signed to cash. But we don't have it, so we make do and do what's supposed to be doing. Like getting up on Sunday and hearing the good word. Where do you take the child?" Mrs. Flynn says.

"First Baptist in Harlem. It's my church." Auntie smiles.

"So far? You know you're always welcome down at St. Anne's with me and the Mrs. It's Catholic, but we all come to the same point, don't we?" Ducks's grandmother laughs to herself, hoping Auntie will join in, which she does.

"I appreciate that and maybe we will, but we have to get on the train if we want a good seat. Come on, baby, let's go," Auntie says, sweeping me in her big arm and waving goodbye to Ducks's grandmother, who walks in the opposite direction.

We race to catch the train and almost miss it, but I hold the door open and Auntie gets on just in time. Luckily there are seats, and grabbing one, Auntie sweeps me over again close to her.

"Mrs. Flynn's nice," I say when we finally sit down.

"She seems it," Auntie says, smiling at me.

"We don't really have to go to mass with her, though, do we?" I laugh.

"No. But it would be a nice thing, maybe. And I love Catholic churches. When you go in, they're always pretty to look at."

"But we're Baptists, wouldn't it be silly to go into a Catholic church?" I say, sort of laughing and still trying to make my auntie happy with me.

"Well, baby, I'm a Baptist. But it doesn't make any difference, really. It's the ritual about it."

"Well, there's more to it," I say. "I mean, like, God."

"Oh sure, if you believe that stuff. But I don't."

"What?" I ask, looking up. I don't understand her at all at this moment. It's all so confusing. What is she talking about? Why are we going to church all the way in Harlem and getting dressed up and then yelling about it, if she doesn't believe in God?

"Well, I'd like to think maybe there's something. But it's not some old white man with a beard, I can tell you that much," Auntie says, laughing to herself. "But I go to the church for something else.

"I love the music. And the people. I guess it's mostly the people," Auntie says. "The old women, wearing their crowns, proud, maybe it's the only day in the week they can feel any pride. And the care they bring into that building, the way they believe and believe in one another just for being there. There's something very holy to that, which probably has nothing to do with God."

"But you say the prayers and call out and sing along," I say, trying to understand.

"Sure. I will today just like every time before. But that's because I want to be part of it. I want to participate in this tradition. I want to go to a service like my mother and her mother and her mother and her mother did before her. I want to be connected to who they were and where I come from. I believe in that. Even if I don't believe in the rest. Still, I don't think it's ever a bad idea to sit in a room with people and think about how to be kinder to one another, do you?"

"I guess not," I answer, more confused than I was before.

"Sometimes you do things for the sake of others, even the ones that are gone, long gone. And sometimes you have to do the right thing for yourself, while you're here." Auntie smiles and pats my face. "Are you warm enough?"

"Yes." I smile back at her.

We ride the rest of the way to 125th Street without saying a word. We get out and walk the blocks over to St. Nicholas Avenue and race to the front, where all the older ladies are saving us a seat. They're happy to see us, especially me. They're glad I came back. I am too.

CHAPTER 21

Allegra doesn't ask about anything besides me and Ryan, but she's never really happy about it. I try to mention other things, like how our project for Mr. Gennetti's class is coming up, due in, like, a week, but she just sticks to her favorite subject, Sopher. That's her couple mash-up name for us. I hate it.

"Well, you and Ryan, Sopher, will probably go as something together for Halloween, won't you?" Allegra asks.

"No. We haven't said," I answer. "And I don't see why we have to."

"Well, you probably will," she says, almost rolling her eyes, and walking away. "You're a *we* now." Allegra smiles this terrible smile like she's caught me in something. But I don't know what. Later, when Ryan and I sit to take a break from walking home and kiss a little, I bring it up.

Ryan puts his arm around me, to keep me warm, I guess. I scrunch down a little to get under his arm and lean on him.

"So about Halloween?" I ask, cupping my mouth on his arm.

"Brian's party," Ryan says.

"It sounds fun." It doesn't, but I'm trying to get to more important things. "What about costumes?"

Ryan's still thinking about going as a zombie doctor. "I was figuring you could go as my zombie nurse."

"Oh, well I thought I would get to decide. Besides, I wanted to go as Daphne from *Scooby-Doo*, I already found this cute vintage dress," I say back to him. "It was in the window of Shelley's, and I have enough money to buy it."

"Oh, but will anybody get that, if you're just Daphne by yourself?" Ryan asks.

"I don't really care about that. Do you?" I ask him. He looks like I've knocked the wind out of him a little. He's so confused by what I'm saying.

"I just don't get what the big deal is. I mean, why can't you do, like, one thing for me?" Ryan pouts and takes his arm off me. I'm the one that's shocked now. One thing? I do lots, and I know it probably sounds silly but this matters to me. I care about things as frivolous and vintage dresses from a store I love and never really have enough money to buy anything in. It's a big deal to me. And he would understand that if he ever asked me anything about myself.

Ryan gets up and puts his hand out to me. "I just thought it would be fun to go together as something. But it's cool." I take his hand and walk with him to my gate. We don't say much after that, and it's probably for the best.

I get into the house and drop my things right at the door. I walk into the kitchen, unbuttoning my coat and really just wanting a glass of orange juice. It's been a crazy day. The kitchen is quiet, and being here, alone, I start to look around me, realizing then that I actually am alone. Auntie's not here. I forgot she had class tonight. And I really wanted to talk to her. Especially now. So I call the next best person I can think of.

"How's the boyfriend?" Ellen says, even before she says hello.

"Don't you start too." I laugh. "I don't know, I mean, do you like him?" I ask.

I can almost see Ellen smirk through the phone. "Do I have to?"

We both laugh at that, but I think for really different reasons.

"Ryan's nice to you. Isn't he?" Ellen asks me, like she can tell from my laugh that something is up.

"No. He's, like, super nice, it's not that," I say.

"Then what is it?" Ellen asks.

I tell her what's it like with Ryan. How he's sweet and nice to me, and pretty much always does the right thing, or does the good thing. It all seems correct, but it doesn't seem right. Like when you solve a problem in math, it all works out perfectly. There's something that's flawless about that, and orderly. That's *right*. *Correct* is something that just works, waiting to be something better. But with Ryan, it doesn't ever feel like that. It doesn't feel right. It doesn't feel solved. It feels like a lot of work for something that's never going to work out anyway. I tell her about the fight, if it even was that, on the walk home, and the Halloween costume problem. Which sounds ridiculous when I say it out loud.

"It's not. It's what you're into. He should be cool about it," Ellen chimes in. "It sounds like you're just not that into him."

"I don't know. Maybe I'm not." I sigh. "I mean, have you ever liked anybody?"

"Well, Charlie, but that doesn't count." Ellen snorts. Charlie was a guy from Ellen's soccer camp who she had over a bunch this summer.

"Why doesn't it count?" I ask right away, because I never even heard this.

"Charlie's super gay. He told me," Ellen says. "He told his mom and dad, and his dad made him go to soccer camp I guess as, like, a last attempt to make him straight."

"Oh, that's terrible," I say back, trying not to laugh.

"I know, and he's really good at soccer," Ellen says, bursting out laughing so I finally get to.

"You know, Allegra thought Ducks was gay," I spit out. I said I wouldn't tell anyone because I think Allegra was a little embarrassed, but that's her thing, and this is Ellen.

"I heard," Ellen says. She tells me how weirded out Ducks was about it and how for the next week, he kept asking her if anything he was doing, like holding a fork or walking down the street, looked gay.

"I felt bad. I thought he was going to have a nervous breakdown."
We both can't help but giggle.

"It's just one thing," I say, trying to defend Ryan a little. "I mean, he's nice in so many other ways."

"But if he's not listening to you? That's more than one thing," Ellen says. "If you like someone, you want to see them happy, right? Well, part of that happy is knowing what makes them happy. If he's not even asking, what's the point?" It's weird to say, but in this moment, I think Ellen is the oldest and wisest person I've ever known. Then she burps real loud into the phone and says, "At least that's what Wendy Williams says."

I can never help but laugh with Ellen. She's that sort of person to me.

"I don't know," I just say. "Maybe it's fine."

"Or it isn't," Ellen says. "And that's fine too. If you don't want to be a zombie nurse, which, barf, and you don't want to be at Brian's, come hang out with us. I have to take Hannah around to trick-or-treat. Ducks and Charlie are coming over. So we'll be here."

Just the words of that plan sound better to me. Being with people who love me and want me to be exactly who and what I am sounds like the best night in the world. I wouldn't even need to be Daphne or a zombie nurse. It wouldn't matter, I could just be myself.

CHAPTER 22

"So, it's almost time for your big Day of the Dead project. I know you're all practically finished," says Mr. Gennetti, grinning to himself as we all settle into our seats. "I thought it would be a good time to take a break from the Phoenicians to start talking about 'our' history. Has everybody at least chosen who they want to be?"

Half the class shoots their hands up in the air. Some of the girls are even fluttering their fingers to show off to Mr. Gennetti how far along they are. I think about lying for a minute and just sticking my hand up, but I don't. I still don't even have a clue about the whole thing. I have no idea who I want to be.

"Well, for those of you who don't, let's talk about options, and maybe we all will get a better idea what the project is about." Mr. Gennetti smiles at the class and sits on the corner of his desk.

"So my mother's name is Rosalie, and her parents came from Puerto Rico." The way he says this, he acts like we've never even heard of the place, mystical Puerto Rico. "Now, does anyone else have family from Puerto Rico?"

A few hands go up around the room, and he calls on Christina Vélez, who stands up, who knows why, to tell everyone in the class that her whole family is from Puerto Rico and they go to the parade every year. Mr. Gennetti smiles and says he loves the parade too. Christina's face looks like he just said he loves her. She gets a little red and sits back down in a hurry.

Mr. Gennetti gets up and walks through the room. "What are the things that make you proud of being from a place?" Rebecca Phillips says history, Mr. Gennetti agrees. Tyler Wendell says music, Mr. Gennetti says sure, and keeps walking.

Ellen waves her hand hard, which is weird, because she's usually never in a hurry to do anything in this class, then she says, "Well, like, what the people there have been through." Ellen doesn't even mumble it.

"That's a very smart answer, Ellen." Mr. Gennetti smiles and walks back to the front of the class. "How a people or a culture survive and go on is a huge reason to be proud.

"The purpose of this project is to show to the class something important about who you are and who inspires you. Does that make sense to everyone?" Mr. Gennetti asks. And while most of the people around me nod like they understand perfectly, I don't, and he notices.

"Sophie, you seem a little lost," Mr. Gennetti says.

"No," I answer. "It's just, how would I even know who to pick?"

"Well, that's really up to you. I mean, the field is pretty open, don't you think?" Mr. Gennetti says. Some girls start to laugh because they all want to please him, which means making me look like a dummy, and that makes me feel worse. But I do actually have a question.

"But, like, what if you're lots of things?" I ask.

"Tell us more about that, Sophie," Mr. Gennetti says.

"Well, it's just, like, I'm a girl." Jeannette Miller snickers from the first row, but I continue. "And I'm black. My mother and her family are black. And my father is white. And I live in Brooklyn, and I'm an only child, and there's lots more, I guess. But how can I, like, pick one thing to be, and come in and talk about how I feel pride about just that one thing?"

"Well, hold up for a minute, Sophie." Hands fly up as soon as he stops me, I guess other people aren't as confused as me. But Mr. Gennetti continues on his own. "See, the thing I think you're missing is that being proud of one thing doesn't take away from other things. You have so many wonderful worlds you get to be a part of, they're all a part of your story."

As soon as he says the word *story*, I start to understand a little.

"Does that help, Sophie?" Mr. Gennetti asks.

Craig Estraga raises his hand and spits out, "And they don't need to be dead, just checking."

A few girls laugh again, and Mr. Gennetti says, "No, they can be alive. It's a day to remember our families and our ancestors and pay them a little respect. But I'm letting you pick any member of your family, living or dead, for the project."

He talks more about the project and takes a few more questions, mostly from kids who have already started theirs but just want to check in that they're on the right path. Hillary Brightman asks if she can bring in spaetzle, which is some weird German noodle thing that her grandmother makes, for the whole class. I have so much to think about, I can't wait to get out of here. As soon as the bell rings, I dart out of my desk and into the hallway.

I run over to Mrs. Wren's room, where Allegra is getting her bag together and looks like she's been crying.

"Hey. What's wrong?" I ask her. This is how I start most of our conversations now. Mrs. Wren watches us, pretending she's not, while she erases the dry-erase board.

"It's, like, seriously nothing, like, at all," Allegra says, putting her backpack on her shoulder, hiding her face from me.

"Are you crying?"

"No." Allegra glares at me.

"Okay, so I'll meet you outside after last bell?" I ask.

"Sure," Allegra says, moving into the hall.

I have to leave a note for Ryan. This is all getting to be too much, all of it, and I need at least one part to stop. I write, *I need to talk to you after school*, and I try to run it over without anyone noticing. But Angela Babiak and Casey Lubeck whoop and "aw" at me, for slipping a note to my boyfriend. I give them a dirty look and get into class—I don't have time for them either.

⌀⌀⌀

After school, Ryan is waiting for me, like always, right by the door. He looks so freaked out and a little scared. He knows something is up. I want to lie, I want to make up some excuse or some story so he doesn't actually feel bad about himself, or like I am choosing Allegra over him, but that is exactly what I'm doing.

"Hey, what's up?" Ryan smiles at me, worried.

"I can't walk home today," I blurt out.

"Why? What happened?" Ryan says, his face sinking. "Is this about the Halloween thing?"

"I just think I need to spend a night with Allegra. I've been ignoring her and I don't want to do that," I say so fast it's even hard for me to understand it, and I'm the one saying it.

"You can't see her tomorrow or something?" Ryan asks, getting closer to me, probably thinking that a kiss will definitely sway me in his direction, but I step back.

"No, I have to go tonight," I say. "I'll text you, okay?"

Ryan stands there. He's upset, I know that, but I just keep moving away until I find Allegra, and we get into a taxi and go. Allegra's quiet for most of the ride, and I am too. I keep thinking of Ryan and feeling bad about it. I wish things were back to how they were before. Back to normal.

It's weird to think that, though, because things getting back to normal would mean Janet coming back and everything that comes with it. I just never really thought, like, regular life, without a drunken mother at home, was all this complicated. The bottom of my stomach starts to hurt, like I'm hungry but different. I think to myself that I'm getting my period. I bet that's part of it, and I'm going to Allegra's. I don't even know if she'll have anything. I mean, she's a girl, so of course she will, or at least her sister will.

"Leg, do you have a thing?" I say.

"What? Oh gosh, are you all right?" Allegra looks up from her phone with a frown.

"Yeah, I'm fine. I just need one."

"Oh, we totally do in the house. Like, if I don't, my sister does, or my mom. Don't worry."

Her sister does and, luckily, is so sweet and cool about it to me. I think it makes her like me even more. And Allegra like me even less.

After about an hour on the iPad, Allegra finally asks me, "Are you going to Brian's Halloween party?"

"I'm supposed to with Ryan, but I don't know."

"*Why?* It's, like, going to be easily, like, the best party. And you're going with your boyfriend. That's, like, the Best Evah," Allegra says, looking at her screen but getting mad at it. Or at me.

"I just don't know if I want to go."

Allegra looks up for the first time. She's annoyed with me.

"He does nice things for you and thinks you're pretty. Like, what is your problem?" Allegra says, standing up from her desk and coming over to me. "I don't get why you're, like, crapping on Ryan like this."

"I'm not crapping on Ryan like anything. He's super nice, but that doesn't mean I have to do everything he says," I tell her, looking up at her. "I don't want to be a girlfriend like that. It's not my thing."

"No, it's not," Allegra says. "You're being a bad girlfriend. Like, you can just go along with stuff, because it's worth it."

"Why is it worth it?" I start to get agitated at her and a little loud.

"It's, like, worth it to have that person. That person who thinks you're smart and funny. To have that one person that thinks you're pretty," Allegra almost screams.

"It's just a party, Leg," I answer.

"Not for some of us," Allegra says, almost starting to cry. "If you don't go, I can't go."

"What are you talking about?" I ask, more confused than anything.

Allegra doesn't look up from her iPad, but it all starts to make a little sense. Brian didn't invite her. That's probably why she was crying today. They have that class together. I didn't think he would be that rotten, but it is Brian so I guess I shouldn't be too surprised.

Allegra wants to say more, I can see it. She wants to tell me how disappointed she is that Brian doesn't like her. Or that she really tried. Or that she doesn't understand why. And for the first time, I see Allegra isn't over it at all. She's deep in it, and she's scared. She's scared she'll never be as cool as her very cool sister. Or as pretty as she thinks I am. She may never be the person who gets someone who thinks they're smart and funny and worth it. Because deep down, I don't know if Allegra even thinks she is. She's scared, and in the weirdest way I feel closer to her than I ever have before. I'm scared too, I just wish we could talk about it.

But then she says, "I think I just need to have a night to myself."

"Are you sure?" I ask her.

"Yeah. I can call you a car home, if you need one," she says, getting back on her computer. But I say I can walk. I grab my things and walk to the doorway to say goodbye, but she doesn't even look up at me, so I just leave.

CHAPTER 23

Auntie Amara takes me to lunch and the bookstore on Saturday afternoon.

She goes around the bookstore slowly, looking at every table and turning over different books from each. She knows about so many different things. I like following her around, amazed at all the things she picks up and trying to guess what she'll pull next. She goes after something flashy with gold lettering and then next she's on to something with just black-and-white pictures on the front. I try to guess the subjects, and there's a little of something from everywhere. History. Romance. Science. Politics. She seems to want to know about everything, I want to know everything about her.

"Have you ever read this?" she asks, picking up a book with a pretty little black girl on the cover with an old-fashioned hat. "It's by Toni Morrison. Do you know her?"

I take the book from her hand and turn it over to look at the old woman on the back. She has long dreads, like Auntie's, but gray and white. Her eyes are open and wide, and she's looking out at you like Auntie looks out in the morning with her coffee. It's a look that knows something, but doesn't tell you. Maybe that's why you have to read the book.

"I'll buy it for you, if you want. Or I have a copy at home. I'll just give you that," Auntie says, taking the book back and putting it on the table before she moves on to the next. She buys three books of poetry, a book on Syria, and another book a lady wrote about growing up in Chicago. She heads over to the wall of journals and picks out one, then waits for me to follow after her as she sweeps through the store.

"Pick one for yourself. I want you to write," Auntie says to me over her shoulder.

"Write what?" I ask.

"You say things sometimes," Auntie says, "that make me laugh, girl. But laugh in a way that makes me know you're thinking. You have a mind. And I think you should give that mind a little space. What about this space?"

Auntie picks up a pinkish notebook with the outline of a girl reading a book on the cover. There are swirls around her and some of them are coming out of her head. It doesn't look like she's writing at the moment, you can't see a pen, but I imagine it's there. I like it, but I want something different. On the side is a thick black book that looks grown-up, serious in a way. I pick that. Auntie asks if I want anything else, and I immediately go and grab a big copy of *Vogue*.

It'll be nice to have a "rag" around again. We used to get it delivered to the house, but Janet didn't renew our subscription.

"Any plans tonight? With your boyfriend?" Auntie smiles.

"He's not my boyfriend," I say, almost without thinking.

"Oh, did something happen?" Auntie says, putting her hand on my arm.

"No, I just don't know if I want a boyfriend," I say.

Auntie Amara laughs so loud, the two girls whispering nearby and a man with a flower brooch laugh back.

"Where did you come from?" Auntie asks jokingly. "You don't want a boyfriend? You're not like your mama, are you?"

No, I think, *I'm not.*

"It seems like so much work. And I have to do things that he wants to do."

"What sort of things?" Auntie chimes in right away.

"Oh, like stupid things," I say, trying to get back to the point.

"He's not doing more than you're ready for, is he?"

"No, not like that. I mean, we kiss," I say, and instantly regret it. But she doesn't flinch.

"And he holds my hand, and I like that. I really do. I just don't know if I like the rest."

Auntie Amara looks at me quizzically. "The rest?"

"Like the having to run things by him, or, like, matching for Halloween."

I tell Auntie about the parties and everything, and all she can say to me is, "You're breaking up with this boy over a Halloween costume. That's cold."

"I didn't say I was breaking up with him." I try to laugh it off, but I'm getting annoyed. "I'm saying that I have enough people. I have you and Ellen and Allegra, and Ducks, and Janet when she gets back, and none of them expect me to change for them."

Auntie laughs again, loudly. "I'm proud of you. Real proud," Auntie says when her laughter quiets down. "So what are you going to do?"

I don't know. I just don't.

The next morning, Auntie falls asleep on the train up to Harlem. She snores a little every couple of stops, but luckily she wakes herself up. I'm happy for the quiet, and for most of the ride, that's all there is. I'm not thinking of anything, just her snore and the rush of the train.

In her apartment, I stare at the picture of Janet and their mother, the one Auntie took.

"Why didn't Janet," I ask, "why didn't she ever take me to see your mother, or at least let me talk to her on the phone?" I spit the words out, getting angrier than I thought I would be.

Auntie looks up and sighs. "It was complicated between Janet and our mother. More than complicated, hard. They were too similar, I think, but neither would ever admit that. Janet was her favorite, and she scrutinized everything your mother did because your mother was the pretty one.

"Janet hated that, hated being picked at and pawed over, and my mother never let up. Everything she ever did had to have my mother's full approval, and rarely did anything ever make it that far. Oh God, they would fight.

"My mother hated that Janet wanted to be a writer, then hated the fact that she wrote about fashion and culture, then hated that she traveled, and then hated your father. She didn't even go to their wedding. None of us did. I couldn't afford the flight to Paris."

Why did Grandma hate my father? I want to say, it's not that I don't get it, but I want to hear the real reason, which I might already know but need to hear to know that it's actually true.

"She didn't want her daughter marrying some white man, and a French one at that." Auntie nervously tries to laugh but stops. "My mother had no time for white folks, none at all. But it was more than that. She hated that Janet was having a life she couldn't have. She resented her for it. Which is a terrible thing for a parent to do to any child."

For a minute, I breathe in and think about this woman hiding her smile from the camera and think about her hating me. About her never wanting to see me, blaming me for something that is nothing I did, but just something that's part of me, and for a minute it makes me feel as angry and as mad as when that lady looked at me and Ryan holding hands near the park. But it's not the same. It's a lump in my throat, but I swallow it and listen.

Auntie's tearing up a little. She puts her hands on my shoulders and walks me over to the couch. She sits down, looking mostly at her hands and glancing up at me, nervous about saying something.

"Baby, I know the hard time you've had with your mother," she says, wiping her eyes. "It breaks my heart to think you had to go through that alone."

Auntie starts to cry, full tears, and I move closer to her on the couch, almost crying a little myself. It makes me so sad to see her like this.

"And I can't let you go through that again," Auntie says, patting tears away from her face and looking right in my eyes. "What would you think about coming here to live with me?"

"When?" I say.

"Starting today, if you wanted. We can go home tonight and get some of your things and bring them up here. There's not a whole lot of room, but we can figure it all out. The couch folds out and I can sleep out here, give you the bedroom."

"But what about school?" I ask.

"We could transfer you to a school up here in a couple weeks." Auntie smiles. "There's a great private school that I think you would love, that's near the top of the park. I have a friend who teaches there, and I was talking to her about you."

"What about Janet?" I ask. I haven't even talked to her since she left.

"I don't honestly know what shape she's coming back to us in. She has a lot on her plate, and I think it would probably be the best for both of you to have some time apart. At least until things get sorted out."

I have a million questions. They all swirl around in my head, about my house, my clothes, my school, Ducks, and Ellen, and Allegra, and Ryan, all of them, and even me. Will I make new friends? Will anyone like me here? Will I ever go back to Brooklyn? Will I ever want to? But all I say is:

"Yes."

CHAPTER 24

Opening the front door, I can finally put my bag down and plug in my phone to check my messages. Ryan's sent a bunch, mostly asking where I am and if I can call him to talk about Brian's party. Halfway through his long blue list of sentences that I haven't replied to, he starts to get nervous and doubt me totally.

I guess you don't want to talk

Hello?

What's up?

Can you text me PLEASE?

I mean, I was away for the day, and look at how he, like, freaks out or whatever. I don't know how he's going to react to the rest when I tell him about leaving tomorrow. I don't want to hurt his feelings, because I do actually like him, I just don't know that I, like, *like* like him. I just don't have the room in me for that.

There's one Bitmoji from Ellen blasting off on her own green farts.

All the rest are from Allegra. She's sorry, she starts off, for the other night.

> You just don't like understand
> because you're like super pretty
> I know that sounds weird to say, but
> it's like so true
> Things are way easier for you and
> they like always will be

I want to call her and scream the truth at her, but I don't. I march up to my room and lie down on my bed for a minute, just silent without thinking of what to do or say to anyone next.

I get up and go into the bathroom, taking my phone with me, and I text Ellen.

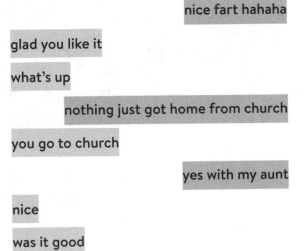

> nice fart hahaha
>
> glad you like it
>
> what's up
>
> nothing just got home from church
>
> you go to church
>
> yes with my aunt
>
> nice
>
> was it good

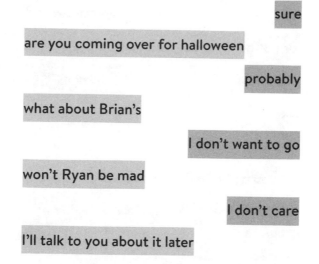

I love Ellen. I really do, because nothing throws her. Like, just then, I probably told her everything I'm going to do, and she doesn't even flinch. Auntie calls up to me to see what I want for dinner. I yell back that I don't care, because honestly I don't. And I move on to Allegra.

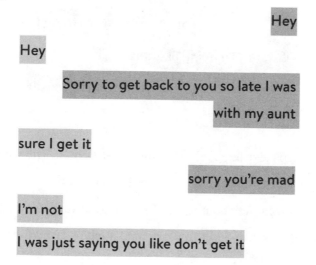

don't get what?

It's not hard for you Sophie

You have no idea

Ok

I'm sorry

are you going to Brian's cause we
should go together

I'm not

WHAT? WHY???

I just don't want to

WHY???

I just don't what's the big deal

why would you ruin this for me

I'm not ruining anything leg

why are you being like this

like what

like a total bitch

She keeps texting, but I don't answer after that. The whole time
I've been friends with Allegra, I've known she has a mean side.
Ducks first told me about it, but I didn't want him to be right. He
also thought she hated him, and the truth is she's dying for him to be

her friend, or anyone to be her friend. But now she's just nuts. How could she say something like that to me?

Auntie calls me down to the kitchen. I'm not even going to text Ryan, that would be too much. I'll deal with him later.

"Don't you need help with that family project? I brought down the scrapbook for you," Auntie asks as we blow on bowls of reheated soup.

"I think I want to go as you." I smile.

"What?" Auntie exclaims.

"We have to go as someone in our family that we're proud of," I say.

"Don't they have to be dead?" Auntie asks, breaking off pieces of bread for each of us.

"No. It's the Day of the Dead, but they don't have to be dead," I answer.

"You sure?" Auntie says.

"Yes. And I want to go as you."

"Well, that's very sweet, baby," Auntie says, touching my face. "And if I had to do it, I would go as you. It'd be a Freaky Friday for the both of us. But I think you should think about going as your mama."

"What? That's crazy." I laugh.

CHAPTER 25

It's starting to hit me that I'm leaving soon, and I don't know how to tell Ducks. He's going to freak out. Walking to school with him, I'm quiet, and of course he notices. I'm still not sad about leaving. That might come later, but I can always come back. It's just a subway ride.

Once we get past the numbered streets, Ducks says, "Ellen told me you're coming over for Halloween. That's cool."

"Yeah," I answer. "What are you going to be?"

"I wanted to do this whole thing with blood and red hair, but I can't. So maybe I'll just put on dog ears and come as Scooby. You're still thinking Daphne, right?"

"That would be funny." I laugh. He does too.

"Why aren't you going with Ryan?" he asks.

"I'd rather spend the night with you guys and Hannah."

"Okay." He smiles.

That's all we say until we're a few blocks from school, and he tells me he likes my necklace. He always says this about this particular necklace, because he gave it to me. When he first started getting into opera, he read something about peacock feathers being a sign of wisdom. Then one day he showed up with this necklace, a single peacock feather hanging from the chain. I knew he'd saved up for it and that it meant something to him. I loved it right away. I wear it all the time, and he always tells me he likes it. I think he's trying to remind me, but I never forget. He deserves to know I'm leaving. Even if it means he gets upset. He does sweet things for me, I should be sweet to him. Even if I ruin his day. So I tell him.

<hr />

"What do you mean you're going to move to Harlem?" Ducks almost squeals.

"I can't stay with Janet anymore," I say. I sigh this long sigh and say, "And I don't want to."

"Why?" Ducks asks. I know he's not registering how my move will affect him at all. He just knows that I'm upset, that something about my mother upsets me, and he wants to know the what, why, and how of it. His feelings will come come later.

"Because I hate it," I say. I'm getting closer to the truth, it's right in my throat, but it's attached to that bubble you have to swallow before you cry, and I'm not sure if I want to cry before school. I breathe deeper and deeper as he asks me a bunch of questions right around the edge of it, and then in one big gulp, I say, "She drinks."

"Okay," he answers.

"She's always drunk. And mean about it. And I have to put her to bed sometimes."

Ducks just says "okay" again and walks closer to me so I don't have to yell it all to him.

"It's been going on for a long time, and it gets really bad, and then she'll try to hit me or . . ."

"She does what?" Ducks asks, almost in tears. He knows what I said, so I don't repeat it.

"Yeah." I smile as the first tear rolls down my cheek.

I tell him all of it, even more details than I gave Auntie. I tell him about locking myself in my room and waiting for her to fall asleep every night, about sneaking the bottles out to Jen in the mornings. But I also tell him how lonely it is, how scary and embarrassing it is all the time. I tell him about the good weeks, when she apologizes, but how I know she'll always go back. For the first time, I say the truest thing I can about it. And he just listens.

"I'm just so tired," I say, almost sobbing, but trying to hold it together.

Ducks puts his face close to mine and is very still. He puts his arms around me slowly, and I put mine around him, we're both crying and trying not to. He knows exactly what I mean. I feel safe with him.

We stand together like this for a while, close and quiet, holding on to each other like we're alone in the world. For a minute I forget that we're on the street and that it's getting late. I don't care, and neither does he. All he cares about is me, and in the moment, that's all I need.

We walk the rest of the way, holding hands and talking about silly things: about the project for Mr. Gennetti, guessing about the Halloween party at Brian's that neither of us is going to, and how we both get caught up or confused in our silly heads, when we know the other one is right down the street.

"I really need to get a phone." Ducks smiles.

We laugh about it, because it's silly and true. When we get to school, we rush to our homerooms but not before he hugs me in the hallway, longer than he probably should. He whispers in my ear that he loves me. Out of everyone, today I needed that from him. He knows me. He's Ducks.

Ryan sees Ducks and me and turns and walks in the opposite direction. He walks as fast as he can without running, but I can tell that he wants to get far away from us and fast. It isn't until after third period that I catch up with him. I follow him to his locker and stare at him until he turns and talks to me.

"What?" he says, not looking at me.

"Can we, like, please talk?" I plead a little.

"Now you want to talk? It's cool, Sophie," he says, closing his locker. "It's fine. You don't like me. I get it. You're a liar."

"How am I a liar?" I ask. I mean I know how I am at times, but he doesn't know that. At least I don't think he does.

"You say you like me but you, like, obviously don't," Ryan says, holding on to his locker door.

I want to tell him I never lied to him, that I did like him. I liked kissing him. I liked walking home with him, and talking to him, and listening to him. It's more about stuff he doesn't know, and I'm sorry for that, sorry that it affects him, but I can't do anything about it. And he should try to understand at least a little.

"Just stay away from me, okay?" he says, finally looking at me.

"Okay," I say.

"Okay." He slams his locker and then he's gone. I walk down the hall and catch Allegra staring at me from the other side of the hallway. She looks sadder than I do. She hurries to close her locker and get away from me. I'm sure she'll talk to me later.

And at the end of the day, just like that, she's walking me out of school.

"I saw what happened. Are you guys okay?" Allegra asks.

"We're not together like that," I answer, walking ahead of her.

"This is all about your Halloween costume? Why not just go as a zombie nurse?" she asks, following me.

"It's not about that at all. I'm not even going to Brian's tomorrow," I say, not turning to look at her. "And I don't want to."

"It's going to be, like, the Best Evah," Allegra says from behind me.

"You can go if you want," I say, not knowing if she's still following but pretty sure she is. I'm the one that's over it now. She can't go without me. I'm sorry for her, and sorry about it, but I'm not going. And she should know that.

Allegra says, "Well, I will." Pushing past me, she gets into a cab. I walk home with Ducks, who doesn't say a word. He doesn't have to.

CHAPTER 26

That night when I get home, Auntie's cooking a big meal. It fills the whole house with the smell of warm paprika and chicken. It's a smell that makes you want to forget everything else around you, and that's exactly what I need.

Auntie talks to me a lot about the move, in a hurried way, like she's nervous someone will hear her, even though it's just the two of us. She tells me about the new school and how soon I will have to get ready to start all over. I need to start thinking about what I want to bring too. There's not a lot of room, but there's enough. She can make space. She will make space for me.

I know it's a lot, but for some reason, I'm not the smallest bit worried. Even when we talk about Janet.

"And when she gets home, I will just lay it out for her," Auntie says, sort of angry but still a little nervous.

"When does she get home?" I ask. It's been longer than any other trip she's taken, and to not have heard from her is really strange. It's also been nice.

"Soon." Auntie Amara half smiles. "Maybe this weekend."

"Well, what does that mean?" I ask, catching some of her nervousness now. "Do we go before she gets here? What are we going to say?"

"I will take care of it, baby. She'll want what's best for you. She'll be all right." Auntie smiles, touching my cheek. "Now let's get started on this project. First, show me how you're going to dress up like me. If that's still what you've decided," Auntie says.

"It is," I answer.

"Well, if you're going to be me, I don't want any pillow stuffing covering your skinny behind." Auntie laughs as loud as she can.

I run upstairs to my room to grab the long white skirt and peasant shirt I was thinking of wearing. I have a few scarves to wrap up my hair, and I'm thinking about letting a few braids hang down from the wrap, just like Auntie always does. When I show her what I'm going to wear, she shakes her head and says I need something else. She takes a strand of her dreads from the back and cuts one off for me.

"Dangle that instead." She smiles.

The little graying tube sits in my hand for a long time. It's so strange to hold a part of another person, but it still feels so very okay. I start writing down her details, leaving the dread at the top of the page as I write.

Dr. Amara Watley, born April 20, 1970 in Baltimore.

Graduated Spelman College in 1992.

Earned her doctorate in 1999.

She writes books and teaches at CUNY.

She's never been married, but she lived with a man for a while.

"I don't know what I think about marriage." Auntie Amara laughs.

For the rest of the night, I ask Auntie about her life, writing down all the details she'll give me. So much of it I don't know.

She tells me how she's trying to make the world a safer, more welcoming place for all women, but especially black women. She says this to me in a much smarter way, but I'm so wrapped up in listening to her that I can't get it down fast enough, when I remember to write at all.

She tells me about school, about her students, and her publishers.

"What are you proudest of?" I ask her.

"Oh, baby, I don't know." Auntie laughs. "Not much I've done. I mean, I write and I get my ideas out there, and I'm proud to have that platform, to be entrusted to speak for people. But what makes me proud is something different.

"I'm proud when a beautiful black girl in my class writes a poem about loving herself. I'm proud when she wins an Oscar or she gets into med school or she can hug her kids tight in her own house and not worry about them being killed by the police.

"And I'm the proudest when she knows her own beauty. Not that I take responsibility for that. I wouldn't."

"Being pretty?" I ask, so confused and only wanting more answers.

"No. Pretty is a dish or a cake, baby. It's something you call an ornament. Beauty comes from what we do, what we have the right and the vision to do and to be. Beauty is how you talk about tools. Pretty is how you talk about Christmas lights."

"I want that," I say, half to myself.

But she hears and lifts up my face with her hand, and says, "Girl, you already got it. You're beautiful to me."

School passes in a flash, with half the kids dressed up in costumes and half not. Everyone's excited about getting out of school and going wherever they can to get candy or hang out with friends. Allegra walks around in a Catwoman costume, telling almost anyone that will listen that she's going to Brian's tonight. It's going to be the Best Evah.

I ignore her because I know it's a show now, or that's she's waiting for me to cave and take her. I know she's thinking the more she tells people and talks up the whole thing, the more I will want to go, but she's just plain wrong. It's almost like she doesn't know me at all.

After school, Ellen, in her plaid shirt and mustache, meets me and Ducks on the street. She's loving being Ron Swanson from *Parks and Rec*, barking out orders at us and being a guy's guy. Ducks won't even put on his dog ears and snout until we get to her house. He has the blue collar and he turns this weird shirt with *Cool Dude* written all over it inside out, because it's brown. He looks something like Scooby, but not really. I'm sort of flattered that he wanted to match me and I'm not even Daphne now.

My costume is good, but not perfect. The purple dress in Shelley's window fit me, and I had enough money to buy it. It just didn't feel like me. It didn't even feel like a pretend me. The red wig was worse. When I tried it on this morning, it just looked so plastic and it covered up my braids, which I love. I decided not to wear any of it. I just threw on some kitten ears and a black dress, and now I'm a kitty. Maybe Ducks and I can still match. He can just be a dog, he doesn't need to be Scooby. He doesn't even seem to notice.

I feel bad for a minute about not being a zombie nurse after all. But the truth is none of that mattered, or mattered as much as I thought. Being heard was much more important.

Ellen's little sister, Hannah, attacks us as soon as we get through their front door. She's so excited about being a ballerina and getting candy that I think she's about to bust right open. She doesn't want to wear her sweater over her tutu, like her nanny, Rosalinda, wants her to, but Ellen makes her. Hannah wants to go now, but Ellen reminds her that we have to wait for Charlie.

"Charlie's coming?" Ducks perks up from the couch. One of his dog ears almost flips up, which makes us all laugh.

"Yes, son. He is," Ellen says in her deepest Ron voice.

On the street, kids are running around, laughing and screaming in all sorts of masks and makeup. We all have flashlights and jackets, but Hannah, without any light, runs the fastest, thinking about all the candy she's soon going to fill her pumpkin bucket with.

Me and Ellen walk together, with Charlie and Ducks right behind us. They're talking to each other a lot, and not in a way that we're invited to hear. Usually Ducks would at least ask what me and Ellen thought about something or how much farther we have to go or how much longer we're going to stay out. But he's just happy talking to Charlie. They're even laughing, and though I'm not invited, it still makes me happy just to be a silent part of it.

I start to worry about Allegra, so I text her.

Hey

Hey

Happy Halloween

Thanks

I'm out with Ellen and Ducks

I think we're going to walk with Ellen's sister and then head back for pizza. Do you want to come?

No. Besides they don't even like me.

They do. They totally do.

It's cool. have fun though.

Ok. Happy Halloween

By the end of the night, Hannah has more candy than she can carry. She's the tiredest and happiest little ballerina you've ever seen. We drop Ellen and her off. Charlie stays with Ellen for a while longer, but Ducks and I ride home together in a cab without saying much. There's not much to say, until Ducks asks, "Are you going to tell Ellen you're leaving?"

"Yeah. Of course. And I'm not, like, *moving* moving, I'm just going to Harlem."

"And a different school," Ducks says.

"Yeah," I say, looking for how close we are to getting home and out of this car.

"I don't want you to go, you know," Ducks says. "But I don't want you to stay either."

I don't say anything but squeeze his hand as we stop in front of his house and he gets out.

"Thanks," I say from my side of the back seat.

"Walk tomorrow?" Ducks asks from the door. I tell him sure.

Even though it's only a few houses away, the car drives me up. The lights in the front room are on, which means Auntie must be waiting for me. That makes me so happy, I run up the front stairs two at a time.

I run in the side door with a big yell. "I'm home." But something's different. Even something in the air is different.

"Baby, come in here," says Janet from the living room.

CHAPTER 27

I walk toward the doorway of the front room, slower than I ever thought it was possible for any person in the world to walk. I look down, hoping that when I get to the doorway, someone else will be there. Someone besides Janet. Anyone else.

My feet move slowly, but inside my head is racing around with everything that will go wrong if it is her. I'll never get out of here. I'll have to face Ryan every day until he calms down and decides not to hate me anymore, whenever that might be. Maybe he and Brian and all the rest of the boys in my class will start to hate me, and somehow even Ellen will have to hate me too. Actually, no she won't. She'd probably like it, because it would give her free rein to hate everyone in our school but this time with an actual reason. And Ducks would still love me. Maybe that'll be enough. Allegra's already gone. I'll fail my project for Mr. Gennetti tomorrow because the minute Auntie leaves, Janet will pull out a bottle, and I won't be asleep until three in the morning. I knew I couldn't get away. I knew it. And when I finally get to the doorframe and look up, it's her.

"Oh, baby, come here," she says, sort of crumpled up on the couch and smaller than I remember. She's trying to wipe tears off of her face as she keeps talking to me. She's waving me over to her, but I don't move. Auntie starts to wave me over, too, but I don't move for either of them.

"It's all right. It's all right," Janet says, looking down into her hands. "I don't blame you. I don't, Sophie." She takes in a very big gulp. Her whole face is shiny and wet. "I'm so sorry, Sophie. I'm so very sorry."

Okay, I mouth, barely loud enough to hear it myself.

Auntie pats Janet's leg and puts her hand on her shoulder. She looks at me hard, pulling me over to them with her eyes. But I still don't move. I can't and even if I could, I wouldn't want to.

"Sophie, say something to your mother," Auntie says, looking at me even harder.

"I didn't know you were coming home today," I say, mostly looking at Auntie and even directing the comment to her. "You never even called once."

"We couldn't," Janet says, twisting her mouth down in a big frown, and she starts to cry again.

"In Paris? You couldn't?" I answer, not flinching about the tears.

"You didn't tell her?" Janet looks over at Auntie, who raises her hand and shakes her head. "You should have told her."

"You told us all not to," Auntie says louder, overlapping me as I keep asking, "Tell me what? Tell me what?" until finally I yell, "Tell me WHAT?"

The whole room stops, and they both look at me a little shocked, but not angry.

"I wasn't in Paris," Janet starts to say, clearing her throat. "I was in rehab."

"She hasn't had a drink in almost thirty days," Auntie Amara says, softer than before, but still eye-pulling me toward them.

"Okay," I say, just looking at Janet. She's crying more than she's looking at me, and I want to catch her eyes to see if she's actually telling me the truth. To see if this is just her being good for us so Auntie will leave, and then in another week, she'll be down in the kitchen having a bottle of wine with dinner and screaming about how ungrateful I am.

"It wasn't okay, Sophie. It wasn't," Janet cries at me. Her eyes are red and lost. She acts like she doesn't know where she is. She's looking for the right way to be but can't find it. When she makes eye contact with me and looks me straight in the face, I somehow know she's telling the truth. I see that whatever she is feeling is real, it's not just a lie till the next drink. This time she means it.

Auntie rubs Janet's back and wipes her dripping eyes. Janet's almost like a baby, she looks so small and weak. I should feel sorry for her, but I can't, not yet; that's how she gets you. But looking at her, I don't actually think she's trying to get me. I don't know what to say or think. And I am a liar. I know that now, just like her. This whole time, I've been telling everyone who will listen that I don't miss her and I'm glad she's gone, but that's been a lie. I always missed her, and I want to hug her and tell her so, but I don't.

"I saw what I was doing to you," Janet says. "I hated myself for that. When I woke up that morning and saw everything I'd done, everything I'd been doing, I didn't want to hurt you anymore. Sophie, I never wanted to hurt you. I love you."

I want to answer her but can't.

"Amara's told me about taking you up to her house for a while," Janet says, calming herself down. She squeezes Auntie's hand, starting in again. "And I understand if you want to go. I understand that it's going to take you a while to trust me again. I understand why you don't now. But I'll be going to meetings and staying in touch with my sponsor. I'm not going to drink again. I'm not. I promise you that.

"If you want to go, I understand." Janet cries harder again and needs to take a break.

Auntie pats her back and says to me, "You have to make the decision, baby."

I am almost instantly angry. I'm right back to hating Janet again, because either way I choose, it's going to be the wrong choice, and she knows that. It's like she's setting me up. If I choose to go, she'll be all alone and afraid and sad, and she'll start drinking again in no time. And if I say no, I have to stay here with her. Either way she wins.

She's still crying. Curled up on top of herself and needing someone to hold her or prop her up straight. I should go to her, but I don't. I don't move. It's almost like when you're a kid and you have that stupid thought that if you stand very still everything will stop. Time will stand as still as you are, but it never works.

"I need to think about it."

Janet looks like she's trying to swallow a big pill. Auntie Amara gets up, saying there's food in the kitchen. She brushes my shoulder as she walks past me to go to the kitchen. She leaves me standing there just looking at Janet, and Janet at me.

I don't smile, I just stare. She's too beaten up to smile.

"You've liked having her here, haven't you?" she says.

"Yeah."

"I knew you would. She loves you very much," Janet says.

"I know," I say.

"And so do I."

Auntie calls us into the kitchen for food. For most of the dinner, Janet eats with a spoon that looks too big for her mouth. She asks me about school. I tell her about the project and going as Auntie. She smiles a little at that and asks me to show her what I look like as Amara. Auntie laughs and tells me to go too. As I run out of the room, I hear her whisper to Auntie about my braids. She likes them.

I run up the stairs and into my room. This is the first time that my mind is actually quiet. I'm not thinking about anything else but getting this outfit on. I take the costume off my chair and slowly put it on. I want it to be perfect, especially perfect, to show Janet. *See, I'm proud of her, I am. And not you.* I wrap the scarf around my head and dangle the dread that Auntie gave me from the front just like it's a stray that's fallen in my face. Like I'm Amara and not Janet.

I run downstairs to the kitchen and catch them hugging hard near the stove. Auntie's eyes twinkle when she sees me, and she starts to laugh. Janet turns around and looks at me. She smiles so big, showing so many teeth that she's embarrassed by them, and she covers her mouth before she begins to laugh.

"You look beautiful." Janet smiles. She rushes over to me, and without stopping, she tackles me into a hug. She's thinner and bony in her sweater, but she smells like Janet. I don't hug back at first, but the tighter she pulls and the harder she pushes my face into hers, the harder it is to not to put my arms around her. I hug her as hard as I can because I want to believe it, I want to think that all of that is over, but I just don't know if I can.

Later, I head to my room to sleep, for the first time in a long time. Janet stops me in the hallway to ask me if she can sleep on my floor.

"Why?" I ask her.

"Because I want to be close to you," Janet says. I look at Auntie brushing her teeth and getting ready for bed. She's not even hinting at me what I should do. So I say I guess, but I don't know if that's right.

Janet grabs pillows and blankets faster than I've seen her move all night. She runs into my room and lays the blankets down on the floor near my bed. I walk around her and straighten my Auntie clothes for tomorrow, looking at her, watching her, wondering what she's going to do. She just smiles and waits for me to get into bed. She pulls my head to her and kisses me on the forehead. She curls up on the floor and says good night. I lie perfectly still in bed for a long time, looking at as much as I can see of her without making it obvious. She doesn't move. She's still. I watch her until my eyes can't stay open anymore, then fall asleep.

CHAPTER 28

In the morning she's still there. She's barely moved. She's even still in the clothes she wore last night. I try to get out of bed and over to my chair without waking her, thinking I can get dressed in the bathroom, but with my first step, she shakes awake and then looks straight at me. She's not angry for being woken up. She smiles.

"Good morning." She yawns at me.

"I'm sorry to wake you up," I say back, almost right on top of her.

"Do you want me to make you breakfast?" Janet asks.

I tell her I'm fine and rush out of the room into the bathroom to be alone. *Is she going to be like this all the time now? All on top of me? Smiling? What does she need to smile at me so much for? What happens when she stops smiling?*

I rush in and out of the shower and then into my clothes, tying the head scarf as tight as I can and putting the dread back in. I hear her going down the stairs, and already I'm thinking about how fast I can run down, put on my jacket, grab my books, and be out the door before she makes me eat a bowl of cereal with her.

I go quickly back to my room to get a few bracelets and the peacock necklace, tiptoeing so that maybe she won't hear me and will think I'm still in the bathroom. That way she won't be expecting me until I'm halfway down the stairs, and closer to the door before she can call me into the kitchen for breakfast. I slip on my shoes and head to the stairs, bouncing off them, trying to touch them as lightly as I can. It isn't until I'm at the front door that she calls out to me. I stop cold. But just stand there. I look back at her.

"I can't. I have to go to school. Sorry," I say, just opening the door and pushing my way out to the street and down to Ducks's house. Ducks comes down the stairs wearing an old shirt of his grandfather's and a big tattoo on his arm in Sharpie. He smiles at me a second before his grandmother comes down the stairs pulling at his shirt and yelling at him.

"Watch that belt. Don't play with it or lose it," she yells.

She makes a big fuss at me, but I just keep moving away from her. I want to be away from these people now, I just want to take Ducks with me.

He smiles at me but knows that I can't smile back, not yet. We walk fast down the block, and by the corner I feel far enough away from them that I can start to relax. Ducks follows, not asking me anything, at least for a couple of blocks. Finally, he asks if I like his tattoo. I tell him it's great and it looks just like Jock's.

"You remember that?" he asks me.

"Of course," I answer.

When we get into school, everyone in our grade is dressed up. So many strange and wonderful costumes. It's really amazing to see, but we both laugh the hardest when we see Ellen, who's wearing a big black wig and an old-fashioned dress with a bustle. She's jocky and all elbows. Sometimes when she moves her head it takes her wig a second to catch up.

"Shalom, kids," Ellen says, pushing both her hands in the air and waiting to hug us.

Ducks tries to pretend to be Jock, but he can't walk like that as well as Ellen can. For a few minutes it's just a fun game between us and not a project at all. It's just us pretending to be people that are part of us. I try to be Amara, but I really just want to laugh with them. I laugh loudly, so maybe I am being her anyway. Allegra's walking by herself in a fur coat, which everyone stares at, wondering how fancy it is and if it is real. I look at her and smile, but she doesn't look at me.

When we get into Mr. Gennetti's class, he's at the front in a pair of old-man glasses with chalk dust in the hair at his temples. It sort of looks good and funny at the same time. He walks differently, too, and holds his pen like it's a cigarette.

"Good morning, class. My name is Ernesto Dejoya, and I am Mr. Gennetti's *abuelo*." Everybody laughs, even though the girls that always like to stare at Mr. Gennetti when he's his usual self are a little disappointed he'll be hiding behind those glasses today. He only acts like his grandfather for a bit before he starts calling on us to tell him our names and something interesting about ourselves.

Ellen stands up. "My name is Ruchel Nussbaum, and I came to this country in nineteen eleven from Poland."

"Nice to meet you, Mrs. Nussbaum. Were things hard for you in Poland?" Mr. Gennetti asks.

"Sure. I came all by myself and worked in a factory until I could send for my three sisters and mother."

"That's wonderful. You must be very proud of yourself."

"You don't leave any man behind. My little *ketsla*, Ellen, taught me that from *Call of Duty*," Ellen says loudly, and the whole class laughs. Mr. Gennetti turns to me next.

I stand up and start. "My name is Dr. Amara Watley, and I'm a writer and a professor."

"A very famous writer," Mr. Gennetti says. "How did you hear about Dr. Watley?"

"She's my aunt," I answer. The whole class whispers about me knowing someone that Mr. Gennetti is obviously impressed by. "I grew up in Maryland with my mother and father and my younger sister, Janet. I was the first woman in my family to go to college."

"That's just one of your accomplishments, though, isn't it?" Mr. Gennetti asks me, already knowing the answer.

"I've written a few books," I start.

"Amazing books," Mr. Gennetti interrupts me.

"And I teach at CUNY in the city," I continue. "I love teaching, and I love when my students begin to understand themselves through the work we do together."

"Well, that's the point of this whole project," Mr. Gennetti interrupts me again. "I wanted you all to learn something about the people in your family to find out something about who you are. What did you find out, Sophie?"

I wait for a minute, not sure how to answer. There's so much swirling in my head, and the harder and harder I think about it, the further and further away I seem to be from an answer. But everyone's staring at me, so I just say, "I found out that I can be beautiful." There are giggles around the room, but Mr. Gennetti shushes them and leans in to ask what I mean.

"Beautiful is how something is made. Beautiful is how things work together, like a piece of music or a poem. Beautiful is how you take all the things that you are, all the stuff that makes you up, and you put it to good use in the world. How you help people with it, and take care of people with it, and how you create things with it," I spit out, not sure how much of this is Auntie's idea or mine. "Pretty is fine, but that's, like, anything, anything can be pretty when you put it in the right light, but to be beautiful is to have a purpose."

"Well." Mr. Gennetti smiles. "I like that very much."

The class, which had been laughing at me until a minute ago, turns and starts to raise their hands to tell Mr. Gennetti who they are next. I sit down in my seat, and Ellen pats my back.

The rest of the class, I think about what I said, and what that actually means. It's so weird to me that after you say something and put the words out into the world, it means something completely different from when you were just thinking it. It's not necessarily that the words are different, but hearing them, using your mouth to make them and your breath to carry them out to the people around you, makes them seem to mean more, makes them seem more real.

I do want to be beautiful. I didn't understand it before the way I do now. And I'm happy but so sad about it, because I know that I can't go with Amara. I know I have to stay here because I have to do so many things here. I have to fix things with Ryan, not be his girl-friend again or anything but at least let him understand that I didn't mean to hurt him. I have to fix things with Allegra, who's just angry with me because she thinks that I have things she doesn't. She should know better. And for Ellen. She needs me in moments, moments she doesn't want to admit, but she does. And Ducks, he needs me, but more than anyone, he just needs me to be me. And Janet. All of these things are my purpose and that's part of being beautiful.

When Mr. Gennetti calls Ducks's name, he stands up and says, "My name is Padraic 'Jock' Flynn, and I'm a carpenter." He smiles, but I see that his lower lip is stretched wide across his teeth to keep him from crying. He looks over at me in a bit of a panic, but I just smile, letting him know whatever happens, he's doing fine.

Ducks shows pictures of all the places Jock built in Park Slope. Martinetti's. Mantelpieces in big fancy houses. The chairs in his mom's bakery. The shelves where his records go. When he pulls out that picture and sees himself smiling with his happy but dead grandfather, he starts to tremble a little, and without missing a beat, Mr. Gennetti pulls him over and gives him a big hug. Tara looks jealous or mad that she didn't think of crying over her dead nana.

"It's hard to lose these people. But a big part of this project is to tell you that they are all still a big part of you. And they always will be." Ducks pulls away, red-faced and embarrassed. Ellen and I both smile at him, and he mouths the word *sorry* to us.

"You have nothing to be sorry for," I tell him on the walk home.

"I feel like such a baby." He sighs.

"You're not. You miss him, that's fine," I argue back.

"I will miss you, when you go to Harlem," he says, looking at me.

"You would let me go?" I ask, really curious about what he's going to say.

"I don't have to, like, let you go or whatever." Ducks stumbles over his words. "But if you think it's the best thing for you to do, if it's going to make you happy, then you should go. That's all I want."

"I love you, Ducks," I say, putting my arm through his and pulling on his shoulder.

"I know." He smiles. "I love you too."

We walk home arm in arm, pretty quietly after that. I kiss his cheek and leave him at his door, marching up to my house. I should be nervous opening the door to go in, because Janet is home again, and who knows what that means, but I'm not. I have something to do now.

Janet and Auntie are standing in the kitchen, listening to music and talking, when I walk in with something to say. They try to ask me about the project and about my day and tell me how good I look as Amara, but I stop them both.

"I want to tell you something. Okay?" I ask. They both answer that it is.

So I stand there and tell them both what I'm thinking. What I thought about before with Janet, how awful and terrible it was, and how I can never go back to that. I tell them about how the weeks with Auntie have been special and warm, and I've been able to be myself and figure out the tiniest bit of who that is. I tell them about fighting with my father, and about Ryan being mad at me, and Allegra, and today with Ducks. But I know what I want to do, not have to do, because I don't want to feel like I have to do anything about this anymore. I've had to do enough.

So I tell them. And Janet cries and so does Amara, and they both hold me close, and though I don't want to, I start to cry too.

"That was beautiful," Auntie says, wiping tears off my face.

And I know for the first time that it was.

CHAPTER 29

Auntie Amara stays for an extra week, just to help Janet get used to being on her own again. It's the first time I've ever really seen them together, and you can tell they're sisters. They argue like sisters, bickering back and forth. They remember things in parts that the other one fills in and then argue over who is right. They love each other, that's underneath it all, but they fight almost the whole time.

Janet goes to her alcoholics' meeting every day and drinks water and eats lots of Sour Patch Kids, which is new, but I would take that over her drunk any day. She's friendly and smiles a lot, which is strange at first, and even though I understand she's been upset, I get over the crying really quickly. I mean, if anyone has the right to cry, it's me, but I don't. She should stop too.

It gets weird about sleeping though. I want to sleep with Auntie again, at least while I have her, but I know Janet will feel alone, and I don't want her sleeping on my floor again, because that will freak me out.

The first night I got home and told them I was going to stay in

Park Slope, Janet slept on my floor again, but I knew she was cold and uncomfortable. I told her to go back into her room, but she insisted on staying there. Finally I told her she had to go. It was making me nuts. I saw how upset she was while getting up, so I walked her into her room to put her to bed. Auntie was reading, and she looked up and smiled to see us.

"Y'all coming in here now?" Auntie smiled.

And before I can really say otherwise, we are. I sleep between them, Janet to my back, kissing my shoulders and thanking me. Auntie lies on her back and starts to fall asleep, which means she starts to snore. I've gotten used to it, but Janet hasn't, and she tosses and turns from the noise.

"Listen to her," Janet whispers to me.

"I know," I whisper back, not turning around.

"She sounds like an old muffler." Janet laughs to herself.

"Go to sleep," I beg.

Janet tries but can't, and even though I know I should be watching her, I can't help myself and fall asleep. At almost three in the morning, I wake up with a start and jump up in the bed. I pat next to me and can't feel Janet. *I knew it*, I think. I knew she couldn't last, I knew she would sneak out to do something. And I signed up for more of this, how stupid am I? *I'm never going to sleep again, am I?*

I get out of bed, quietly, and try to get to the door without waking Auntie, who is still snoring away. I get to the door and open it slowly till I can just fit around it. There are lights on downstairs, and some soft music playing, but I know she's drinking. I knew this was all a big fake-out, and now I've given up going away with Auntie to start this all over again. How could she do this to me? How?

I get down the stairs, almost without a sound, and walk into the kitchen, where nothing is out of place, the stove's shut off, and all the drawers are closed. She's being secretive about it, because she knows now what getting caught means, she's afraid but she's not sorry enough to stop. She's in her office. I can hear her in there, so I slide a little across the tile in the kitchen so I can get to the door without her hearing me.

"What are you doing?" I ask at the doorway.

Janet is curled up on the couch, reading a book, with a glass of water.

"I couldn't sleep," she says, looking up from her book. "Couldn't you sleep either?"

I don't answer. She knows I couldn't sleep and she knows why.

"Do you want to sit with me a little?" she says, picking up the blanket over her legs and waving me under. I go over and sit with her, looking around the room for what's really going on here. No bottles, no cans, and the door to outside is locked.

"It's hard for me to fall asleep now." Janet smiles. "And Amara doesn't help."

"She can't help it," I chime in.

"I know. That's why I didn't want to wake you two up." She smiles. "Do you have trouble sleeping?"

"I did," I say.

"I see," Janet says, embarrassed and a little hurt.

I can't help that I always want to do this to her but I do. I want her to know how awful it was, how mean and crazy she's been for years, I want to threaten her all the time that if she slips up even the tiniest bit, I'm leaving. I want her to know how serious I am, and that what I say matters now, because for so long, it didn't. I didn't matter at all.

"You know, I like this. I like that you sleep with Auntie and that you invited me in."

"It's nice," I answer.

"We never did that." She smiles.

"We couldn't," I snap back.

"Sophie, I know you're angry at me. I know that, and I know you have every right to be," she says, breathing in deeply. "I'm not going to let you down again. I promise."

"Okay," I answer.

"I hate what I've done to you. You deserve a lot better than me. But I want to take care of you now. You don't have to worry about me. I promise you, you don't."

"I don't know how to not worry about you, Janet," I say right back.

"I know," Janet says, starting to cry a little, but she pulls it back together. "But how about, at least tonight, we take the night off? You don't worry about me, and I just hold you. How's that?"

I want to say no. I want to say a slew of nasty things to her, but I don't. I'm too tired to fight. So I lay my head on her lap and start to fall asleep.

When I wake up again, it's early in the morning, the gray part of the morning before the pink starts, and only a few birds are up to talk about it. Janet is asleep sitting up, with me still on her lap. I get up and away from her for a minute, just to make sure she didn't move. I walk around the room again to look for bottles or something, anything, but there's nothing. It's hard to believe, but I have to.

I walk back through the kitchen and turn off the music she left on all night, trying to head back up to my bed, but by the time I hit the bottom of the stairs, I see Auntie standing in the living room, looking out the windows.

I walk toward her, slowly, not wanting to interrupt this moment she's having but still wanting to be a part of it. I walk up close to her and she doesn't move. She doesn't even flinch, and I look out at the spot I think she's looking at. She takes a big breath.

"We do terrible things to the people we love," Auntie says. "And it's not because we don't love them, sometimes it's exactly the opposite. Sometimes we love someone so much, we forget how to show it. We forget that the little tiny signs of love are the most important parts. Like this."

Auntie swings her arm around me.

"What are you looking at?" I ask.

"I'm just looking. I know what I'm looking at, but I know that it all means a lot more than I can see, and I'm looking for a way in."

"I like that," I answer.

"I knew you would." Auntie sighs. "I'm glad you're staying here. I'm not glad you're not coming with me, but I think you're doing the right thing."

"I guess," I say.

"You just promise me this right now: You have a phone, you use it, if you need anything at all. You're not in this alone anymore, baby."

"I will." I smile.

"See that you do." Auntie smiles and holds me a little closer.

When we finally break, Auntie laughs a little and says, "You certainly do like those beads, don't you?"

I look down at my wrist to see the beads she gave me in her apartment wrapped around my wrist. I didn't even remember putting them on this morning.

I smile back. "They're part of my story now."

"I'm glad to hear it," Auntie says, sipping her coffee and looking back out the window. "Now get to school. Just because your mama's home doesn't mean anything changes."

I head out the door, hoping she's right.

When Sunday comes, I get ready for church, but I know they've been fighting about it. Janet doesn't want me to go to that place, she doesn't like all that stuff, but Amara tries to tell her that it's different. Finally, I have to speak up and say I'm going, that I want to go, and I want Janet to come with us.

Auntie's face almost falls off when I say this last part. Janet hasn't been in a church in almost twenty years and she swore she would never go in one again. I tell them both I don't care. We're going. They both laugh at how bossy I get about it, but soon enough we're all on the train up to Harlem.

Janet's nervous about going, and she mopes when we're not looking at her. But she perks up when she thinks we're upset and tries to make us both feel like it's all right. It isn't, but I don't want to worry about that right now. I just want to go.

The old ladies in the front all make a fuss over Janet, for how pretty she is and how well she's dressed, and when they find out she's my mother, they tell her how sweet and Christian I am every week. Mrs. Threadgood tells Janet right off the bat that she's raised a good girl. Janet says she knows.

Janet starts off slow with the service, she knows the songs and she claps along, but I can see that she doesn't want to be here. She listens to the sermon and nods with the parts she likes but whispers "no" out of the side of her mouth for the bits that she doesn't. She's having a miserable time until later, when a little old lady gets up to the piano and starts to play a song that I've never heard before, but both Janet and Auntie know well.

I don't know what I expected to come out of this little old lady, but when she opens her mouth, this voice, this voice bigger than I have ever heard in my life, fills the church. She's not even looking up at us, it's just her and this music, this beautiful music with lyrics I can barely understand but I can feel. Janet knows all the words, and in the softest way she mouths them along with the little old lady. So does Auntie, but neither are loud enough to be heard. They hold hands like they did when they were little girls in that picture. It's a moment of magic. There's no other way to say it.

When the old lady pounds on the piano and sings, "Earth has no sorrow that heaven cannot heal," Janet gasps, trying to keep the tears in. I know I've been sick of the crying, but in this moment I know it's real and I hold on to her arm. So does Amara. Mrs. Threadgood says the Spirit's won a heart today, and despite herself, Janet nods and says it has.

We leave Auntie outside the church. We hug for a long time. Auntie almost picks me up to get more of me in her arms. She's telling me to call her, to never for a second think she doesn't love me or that she won't be there for me. I'm her baby, and that's always going to be true no matter where I go or what I do.

I don't say much, I'm just trying to freeze the moment in her arms. Trying to remember all her smells and how her skin feels against mine. I want to have all the details of her so I will not ever forget, no matter what. I want more of her, and in this moment, I'm scared I won't ever get enough.

Janet walks me down to the subway, holding my hand. She hasn't ever done this that I can remember, but I like it. She tells me about the song. Her father used to sing that hymn when she was a girl, to teach the girls about mercy.

"My father always said mercy was forgiveness with a little bit of forgetting and a little bit of understanding that you've done something somewhere just as bad." Janet smiles. "I haven't heard that song in forever."

"I liked it," I say. The train doors open, and we race in to try to find a seat. We find two and sit down next to each other. We ride for a while not talking, just holding hands and listening to the sounds of the train.

"I guess it's just you and me now." Janet sighs when we pass through the tunnel into Brooklyn.

"It doesn't have to be," I answer.

We get off at Jay Street to transfer to the F train to take us home. I think I see Jen, down the platform. She's standing with a big pile of books and schlepping the cart her grandmother sometimes uses, but I don't see her grandmother anywhere. I let go of Janet's hand and head down the platform to see Jen, who smiles when I call out to her.

"Hey, where have you been?" I ask her.

"Oh, I don't have to do the cans and bottles anymore." Jen smiles, a little embarrassed that I'm bringing it up.

"Oh, I'm sorry. Where's your grandmother?" I ask, looking around for her.

"She died," Jen says, looking down at the cart.

"I'm so sorry." I'm shocked. It's why she doesn't have to come around anymore. It's why I haven't seen her and why I probably won't see her again. I don't know but I hug her, hard, and before I know it, there are tears streaming down my face and hers. Jen hesitates a little but hugs me back harder still. We hold each other for a long time, probably longer than either of us think we can or want to, but I think we both need to.

Jen looks up and sees Janet coming toward us.

"This your mother?" she asks.

"Yes. But it's fine," I say.

"Good, that's important." Jen smiles.

Janet smiles at us both, and I introduce them.

"How do you know each other? School?" Janet asks.

"No, we're friends," I say quickly, not needing to explain anything more.

The C train pulls into the station, and Jen needs to go. I tell her to come over and so does Janet, but I know that won't happen. I wave to Jen as she gets on the train, and I keep waving until the train leaves the station, knowing that it's a goodbye.

It's cold when we get out of the subway. I take my phone out of my pocket to text Auntie that we've made it back to Park Slope, and there's a text from a number I don't know.

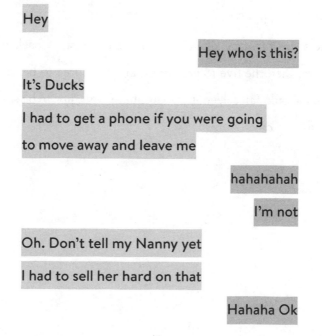

Hey

Hey who is this?

It's Ducks

I had to get a phone if you were going to move away and leave me

hahahahah

I'm not

Oh. Don't tell my Nanny yet

I had to sell her hard on that

Hahaha Ok

I text Auntie and tell her we're home and all right. Going through the door for the first time with my hand in Janet's, I even start to believe it. We eat and watch TV, we fall right back into a schedule with just us together again, and the worry starts to disappear. I still hear something and jump, but I wait to ask what's wrong before I start in running after her. It's getting easier. I hope it stays that way.

That night, I get into my bed early and listen for her.

The water's running. She's in her bathroom.

She turns off the water and I wait to count her steps, but after six, she's at my doorway, looking at me.

"I love you, Sophie."

"I love you too," I say from my bed.

She turns off the hall light, taking the six steps back past the bathroom, then the five to her room, and the three to her bed, and she's in. I should fall asleep, I want to, but I wait, just to be sure. And slowly, day by day, I am.

AND NOW, A SNEAK PEEK
AT JUSTIN SAYRE'S PREVIOUS BOOK
ABOUT SOPHIE'S BEST FRIEND, DAVIS:

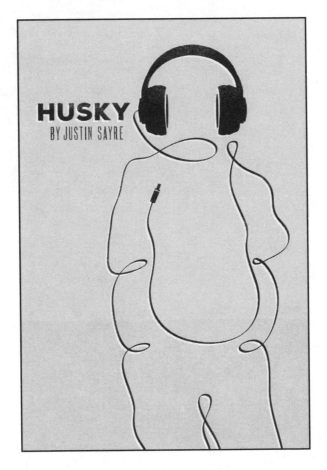

HUSKY
BY JUSTIN SAYRE

AVAILABLE NOW

CHAPTER 1

"Ducks, now would you look at this! Let's just hope they have one in your size."

There's no sound like it in the world. Louder than an ambulance, more annoying than a car alarm, the sound of my Nanny yelling stops me cold every time. Every time. Honest. It's so loud that all the other sounds in the world sort of stop out of shock. So do all the people in earshot, at least all the ones in the Boys' section at Target. Her accent doesn't help. There's just no getting away from it. None. She's talking only to me. I can't shrug it off or pretend I don't know her. I'm the only "Ducks" here. Really, Davis, but Nanny calls me Ducks because I waddled when I first started walking. I don't know that a person should be punished their whole life for how they started doing something, but I am. So to everyone from then on, I have been "Ducks."

No one knows why she yells like this. We used to think it was just at home, with Jock's TV blaring, that maybe she felt like she had to yell over it. But it's everywhere. Mom thinks it's Nanny's cry for attention, like maybe she thinks people aren't listening to her, but that is impossible. Everyone, everywhere is listening to her, whether they like it or not. I just think it's the way she is, Loud. It's not a mean loud or an angry loud—it's meant to be a nice loud. But it's still shocking. I'm never afraid of her yelling, it just embarrasses me and shocks other people.

As I walk over, I see that she's holding just the kind of shirt you would expect a grandmother to like. It's something she thinks is real "hip" or "cool" but is actually terrible in a pretty obvious way and so babyish, I know I'll have to wear it just so I won't hurt her feelings or remind her that I'm growing up, which I am, even though she and the shirt are choosing to totally ignore the fact. This shirt is sort of perfect for that. It's brown with blue "graffiti" lettering all over it saying, "Cool Dude." All Over It. As if one big "Cool Dude" wasn't enough, the shirt really wants to let everyone know from every angle that the person wearing this shirt is a Cool Dude. As far as I know, cool dudes don't need that much advertising.

But Nanny thinks they do, or at least I do, and she smiles this big smile as she holds it up to my shoulders and knocks me in the face with the hanger.

"The shoulders fit, but I don't know about the rest," Nanny says as I try to give her the *Pleasestopyouareliterallykillingme* look through the hanger squishing my nose. She doesn't see the look. She's too happy with herself to notice.

"Well, doesn't that do a wonder for you!" Nanny smiles. "And you're a cool dude, aren't you, Ducks?"

How do I tell my grandmother, no, I am not cool? In fact, I may be Weird. Or maybe Nerdy. Definitely Quiet, which sometimes comes off as a little Creepy.

I'm trying to just be me, whatever that is, but whatever it is, I already know that it's not cool. My friend Ellen, who is Mean but still my really good friend, says before you get to high school you get boiled down to only one adjective. You're the *Sweet* kid or the *Smelly* kid or the *Annoying* kid or the *Rich* kid. One word. One adjective. That's it. It's decided. There. Permanent. And I see that it's true, even now. I mean, in my friends, Ellen is the *Mean* one, and Sophie is the *Pretty* one. One word. And as for me . . .

I'm the *Fat* one, but everyone calls me *Husky*.

Husky is the nice way for your mom's friend or even your mom to call you fat. Department stores too. It's a funny word, and makes you think of a strong dog in Alaska or something else cute but powerful. It's trying not to be as gross a word as *fat*, which just sounds disgusting, but it's still a punch of a word that always hits you right in the jaw. *Fat*. People say *husky* so that they can sort of pat you on the cheek instead of punching you right in the mouth.

But if you know what it actually means, it's all the same thing.

I'm not huge. I'm just, well, *husky*, I guess. I mean, my stomach

227

is squishy and hangs off the sides a little. And I have really thick legs that are strong but look like tree trunks. My arms are thin, and I don't have, like, rolls or anything or a double chin, so I'm not, like, gross or something. And I don't have man-boobs. I'm not even that fat. I'm just sort of, well, husky.

But I don't want to be the *Husky* kid. I don't want *husky* to be my adjective. But trying on clothes, so many clothes, with my loud grandmother shouting sizes at me over and over and over again, proves that I am. I definitely can't be cool like this. So Nanny's shirt would just be a big-brown-with-graffiti-lettering lie. In XL.

"You don't like it, I can tell by the face," says Nanny, finally noticing. "Well, show me something you do like then. We need to get you some clothes."

We do need to get me some clothes, because school starts in two weeks, and I have nothing to wear. I've been putting this off and off and off for the last couple of weeks because, well, besides the yelling, I hate shopping with Nanny. It's not just her, I sort of hate shopping at all, which probably sounds weird, but it's true. I don't really like buying clothes. Because when I buy clothes, and especially with Nanny, I always have to deal with my word. It's not that she makes me feel bad about myself, well, not on purpose. But "Let's hope they have it in your size," what was that? It's a Large, not a Tent. She never *really* says anything mean. She knows who I am and what I look like, and to her those things are fine, and she loves them, because they're me, but I don't want them to be. But also the yelling. A big part of it is the yelling. There's nothing worse than having "You need that in an X-Large, don't you, Ducks?" screamed across a store to remind you and everyone standing around that you are, indeed, *Husky*.

I guess, for at least one more day, I don't want to be reminded that this may be the thing I am known as for this year. That *husky* may be my adjective. Clothes won't help. I sometimes have this weird idea that if I try on an outfit to look a certain way, I'll automatically look that way. If I had a jacket and a tie on, I would be a business guy and my shoulders would be big and my wrist would be thick for a big metal watch and everything would be the way it's supposed to be. Like my body knows how to change with the fabric and it does, and then I am different. I can be that thing, anything, or anyone else perfectly, just because of some clothes. But I can't. Trying on all this stuff today makes me think that whether I like it or not, I am the husky kid. I might not even get the chance to be *Weird*. Or *Nerdy*. Or anything else.

llllllll

I start trying to find something that I do actually like, something to make me even a little different. But again and again, it's all husky. One pair of jeans actually has it written right on them. Gross. Your adjective says really everything about you. Ellen's the mean girl, and that's her. She says sarcastic, but she's not. Sarcastic would mean it's partially a joke, but with Ellen, it never is. It's usually just one mean word at a time. Last year Ellen got braces and started talking out the side of her mouth, like she was trying to sneak the words, which makes a lot of sense, because everything she says is pretty rotten. It's not *mean* mean, but it's definitely not nice. For a while, I thought her braces were too tight and they were squeezing all the nice things out of her mouth. But then Connor Broeckner got braces too and he was fine and when Kaitlin Koecheck got them too and was still silly, I had to think that *Mean* or *Sarcastic* might just be Ellen's adjective. Her braces just sort of turned it up.

Sophie is the *Pretty* one. Beautiful, really. But that's a lot to say all the time. And then people think I'm in love with her or something, when it's not like that. At all. Sophie is my best friend. Or at least she was. I'm not sure, it's been weird lately, and I blame it on the pretty. It's a strange thing how people become pretty. I mean, I always thought Sophie was beautiful because she was my friend. And I always was happy to see her face because it was connected to my friend Sophie, who loves pickles and who had to stop wearing long sleeves for a while because she was constantly wiping her nose on them. This is my Sophie, who's been my friend since we were practically babies, our moms are friends and we live down the block. We know each other. But last year, other people started to be really excited to see Sophie too. More excited than to see me. Then everyone was really nice to her, and some boys, well, a lot of boys, started to *like* like her. It got where every outfit she wore was the right outfit, and her hair was the right hair. And nothing had to change, everything was right because it was on Sophie. People look at her all the time now. Boys who never looked at her before and girls neither of us ever even talked to, like Allegra Bernstein, who is seriously the Worst, have started wanting to be her friend. Everybody wants something from her. Most of the time, Sophie just looks away. The trouble is, she's started to look away from me too. And I don't know why.

It's not all the time.

There are still times when it's just the three of us and it's the same as it was before. We're laughing and kidding around and it's great, but then all of a sudden it's not. Whatever was there, is Gone. I don't know what happens. I don't know where all that fun or what we were goes to, but it's gone, and then Sophie gets really quiet and sort of goes away too. What's left is a girl who looks like my friend Sophie but isn't her at all.

𝓵𝓵𝓵𝓵𝓵𝓵𝓵𝓵

After we pick, well, Nanny picks, about twenty, at least twenty, outfits from the racks, I have to try everything on. Everything?

"Yes, everything. What do you think? They're all the same? Try them on." Nanny laughs as she closes the changing room door.

If I hate shopping, I hate trying clothes on more. Like people hate going to the dentist hate it. You get forced into this tiny little white room with the brightest lights in the world, as if I need to see what these clothes would look like on the sun, and then you have to get naked. Well, not naked, I mean, I keep on my underwear, but still, I'm just in my underwear in a store with my grandmother sitting right outside and waiting for the fashion parade to begin. That's the other thing. Not only do I have to try them all on to see if I like them, I have to try them on to see if she likes them. And she has to check the fit. That means there's a lot of pulling and "fixing" shirts. Adjusting them all while she complains about how fast I'm growing or how they don't size these things right. She adjusts me from every angle, and not easy like fixing flowers, but like let me pull you up by the back of these pants and see if they'll hold. Essentially, Nanny gives me atomic wedgies to see if my pants will hold if I were hung from the ceiling. At least my jeans wouldn't rip. That would be the embarrassing part.

The first outfit, the shirt's not right.

The second, the jeans seem a little too long.

"I'll hem them. Or maybe you'll grow. That'd be nice, wouldn't it?"

The third is right, but I hate the color. Even though:

"That green does a wonder on you, Ducks." She smiles.

The fourth, fifth, and sixth all have pieces that work, but also pieces that don't. *So* there's a lot of tugging and folding and fixing. I go in to try on option seven when she knocks on the door with, "You don't need pants, do you?"

To my Irish grandmother, *pants* means underwear. And to me, underwear is not happening today. Not ever, actually. Not with her.

"No." I hope that somehow she can see my *Pleaseyouare-literallykillingme* look again through the door.

"'Cause we're here, I can go get you a bundle now."

"No. I'm fine."

There's a pause while she figures if she should go and get some anyway, or wait and take me with her to embarrass me, or just not buy them at all. Underwear would be the worst part of an already terrible day. Underwear shopping in general is pretty gross, but with those guys on the underwear packages, the shirtless smiling guys, with the muscles and the big grins, like, "Look how hot and sexy I look in these briefs. If you bought these, you'd be sexy just like me," it's terrible. Nice try, jerks, I've learned that lesson on every other outfit in here. And put on a shirt, we're in a store.

The last time I bought underwear with Nanny, it was awful. Aw. Ful.

"Oh, these with the stripes are nice. Do you like them?" she screamed. "What about the ones with the dogs on them? Does that mean something I don't know? Don't tell me if it does." Then she laughed, thinking I am sure something totally disgusting about people in underwear, or maybe me in underwear, which is so disgusting, it all makes me want to throw up. And then Nanny thought this guy on the package with black hair and a hairy chest was cute, which is gross but totally happens, and said, "Would you look at him. My Word."

My Word is Old Irish Lady for Wowza.

And *Wowẓa* is Me for Barf.

Finally she says through the door, "Fine. But we're here, so if you need pants, it's best to get them now. I won't come back."

Neither will I, don't worry.

ꬹꬹꬹꬹꬹꬹꬹ

When it's all over, I have two big bags of clothes, none of which make me into anything else but the husky kid, even though one shirt insists that I'm a "Cool Dude." Nanny's paying, so she wanted to get something she liked. We spent a lot of money, and that part always makes me feel bad. I really don't need any of this. None of it's going to help.